The Redeemer
A Scarlett Bell Thriller

Dan Padavona

Copyright Information

Published by Dan Padavona

Visit our website at www.danpadavona.com

Although some of the locations in this book are actual places, the characters and setting are wholly of the author's imagination. Any resemblance between the people in this book and people in the real world is purely coincidental and unintended.

The Redeemer

The Redeemer

CHAPTER ONE

Vengeance is the progeny of maltreatment and corruption.

The weather, fair and warm for October along the Chesapeake Bay, should have put Scarlett Bell at ease. Yet something dangerous prowled inside the FBI agent as she paced the beach. Her partner, Neil Gardy, the Behavioral Analysis Unit's dark-haired senior agent, spotted Bell's anger the moment he arrived. Dressed in his work clothes, black suit and shoes with his hair neatly combed, Gardy's clothing was ill-suited for a walk on the beach. Gardy had visited Bell's bay side apartment on her day off, concerned over his partner's wellbeing.

"Any word from Weber on the San Giovanni assassination?" she asked, skipping a smooth-sided rock across the waves.

"Weber doesn't want BAU involvement."

Ever since a sniper gunned down star congresswoman Lana San Giovanni, Don Weber, Deputy Director of CIRG, had lobbied against BAU involvement in the investigation. The murder of political figures fell upon the

4

FBI, and the BAU typically contributed to counter-terrorism and corruption cases, so it confused Bell and Gardy why Weber remained steadfast against the BAU investigating the assassination.

"Weber claims we're stretched thin," Gardy continued, stumbling when the sand engulfed his dress shoes. "His number one priority is catching Logan Wolf, and he wants all available resources devoted to bringing Wolf to justice."

Gardy's words were fuel to the flame, and Bell grew irritable as Gardy justified Weber's decisions. Bell believed Wolf, the former BAU profiler accused of murdering his wife in 2013, was innocent. The murder felt too perfect, too planned for a disorganized, violent serial killer. Wolf had found Renee on the kitchen floor of their Virginia home, throat slashed with a sack placed over her head. Forensic evidence pointed an accusing finger at Wolf. The crime scene investigators uncovered Wolf's prints and hair fibers at the scene, but it was expected. Wolf lived there. The lack of DNA evidence for a third person implicated Wolf, and the profiler had been a fugitive ever since, murdering serial killers across the country to avenge his wife. Worse yet, Wolf adopted the unknown murderer's modus operandi, slicing his victim's throats and placing sacks over their heads to draw his wife's killer out of hiding. But since then, no other killings mimicked the 2013 murder, further proving Wolf must be guilty.

"Nothing changes. It's a waste of resources. Weber can't catch Wolf."

"He will," Gardy said, studying the breakers as the ocean dragged a string of kelp over the beach. "Wolf keeps taking chances by involving himself in our cases. One of these days, he'll walk into an ambush."

Though Gardy had come around to Bell's belief that Wolf might be innocent, she didn't trust her partner to keep their collaborations with Wolf secret. While the fugitive had helped Bell and Gardy track multiple serial killers over the last year, Gardy put honor and duty first. Eventually, Bell theorized, Gardy would lay a trap for Wolf and turn the mass murderer over to the FBI.

"There's something San Giovanni's mother told me at the hospital," Bell said, ducking when a wind gust hurled sand at their faces. She stepped through the waves, prompting Gardy to follow, the agent maintaining a safe distance between the tide and his expensive shoes. "San Giovanni had powerful enemies. The congresswoman headed the task force targeting government corruption. What are the chances she uncovered evidence that got her killed?"

"It's a logical theory, except the FBI couldn't find a connection. Most of the task force's targets were small time offenders: government officials accepting bribes, overzealous lobbyists influencing elections. Nothing particularly juicy."

"Doesn't it concern you Weber kept us out of the loop? It makes me wonder about his innocence."

Gardy stopped along the shore and grabbed her arm.

"Wait a minute. Are you suggesting Weber masterminded an assassination?"

"Weber is involved. He didn't pull the trigger, but I bet he knows who did."

"Listen to yourself. Bell, regardless of your personal issues with the deputy director and the amount of hurdles he puts in your way, you can't possibly believe he's behind the murder."

Bell chewed her lower lip, unconvinced. The sun dropped low, the water turning red as light seeped out of the sky.

"I'm certain Weber would do anything to accelerate his career." Gardy started to protest, and Bell raised her hand. "Let's assume San Giovanni's task force gathered damning evidence against an elected official, someone powerful enough to push Weber up the food chain."

"But they didn't. We saw the notes. The task force investigations are old news."

"Let me finish. The congresswoman was a bulldog, but until she had evidence against an opponent, she played the hand close to her chest."

"So you're suggesting San Giovanni wouldn't bring the case to the task force until she knew it was strong."

"That's exactly what I'm thinking. The FBI hasn't turned over enough stones. I'd check the congresswoman's computer files for—"

The gunshot echoed down the beach. At first, Bell thought the naval jets flying out of Norfolk caused the sound. Then a red streak formed across Gardy's pant leg, and he dropped to his knee, clutching his thigh.

When the second shot tore over the sand, Bell knocked Gardy flat and covered him amid the sloshing water and frantic gulls. She glanced around the beach, searching for cover. The nearest dune lay fifty paces away. Then she saw it. A trench dug around a crumbling sandcastle, just enough space for the two of them to lie flat inside.

Tugging Gardy's arm, Bell coaxed the injured agent toward the trench as another gun blast flew over her shoulder, close enough to raise the hair on her head.

"Stay low," Bell said as the gunfire kept them pinned. "How's the leg?"

"It grazed me. I'll be okay if I can—"

The next shot barreled into the sand, cutting Gardy off. Grit sprayed her face while she covered her head. Protective of her injured partner, Bell shifted her body to shield Gardy's, earning her an irritated groan.

Sirens approached the coast. The gunfire ceased, the sniper fleeing.

Carefully, Bell emerged from the trench, convinced the shooter would pull the trigger now that they'd come out of hiding. Gardy's leg buckled, and she caught him. Blood soaked his pants leg and colored the sand, welling through his fingers where he clutched the wound.

"Can you make it to the building?" she asked.

Bell's apartment complex rose above the beach, a five-minute walk. Longer if a bullet struck you in the leg.

Grinding his teeth, he nodded and limped over the sand with Bell supporting him. With her free hand, she dialed 9-1-1. An ambulance was on the way.

As Bell glanced over her shoulder, a dark figure disappeared behind a dune along the distant shoreline.

CHAPTER TWO

The Florida storm over the Atlantic turned the sunset bloody and flickered lightning like snake tongues.

Christina Wolf sipped a Merlot on her balcony overlooking the ocean as darkness rushed out of the east. The beach house rental was a splurge, a method to unwind and put her work as an information technician specialist aside. She'd survived a messy divorce to Kevin, and Buddy, her Irish Setter of fifteen years, passed in July, leaving Christina alone for the first time since those post-college bachelorette days when her biggest concern was which club to frequent with her friends.

Her job had become a dead end, a compromise. It paid the bills, but she hadn't been excited about work in years. Now at forty, she felt alone in the world. Both parents dead. Her brother, Logan, a fugitive running from the government. The things the media claimed Logan did, the grotesque murders, didn't seem real. She refused to accept her brother was a serial killer. He didn't slaughter men across the United States.

And he didn't murder Renee. He loved his wife.

9

Worshiped the woman. Logan rarely smiled before he met Renee in college. Christina's brother always seemed so serious, so career-driven even as he studied criminal justice. But when Renee entered the room, the corners of Logan's mouth quirked up as though he concealed a joke behind his lips.

She hadn't heard from Logan since Renee's murder. But now and then she returned from work and found differences with her house—someone had tightened the lock on the back door which no longer jiggled, and once someone fed Buddy and left a vase of wildflowers on the kitchen table. She wanted to believe the silent benefactor was Logan, not Randy or Kylie next door, the way a child attributes presents at Christmas to Santa.

And this evening she'd discovered the Merlot wrapped by a red ribbon and waiting on the counter. Kevin hated wine, especially Merlot, and she'd forgotten the pleasures of wine during her suffocating marriage. The only surviving member of her family who appreciated wine was Logan. Still, it was more likely the homeowner left the bottle as a gift and she'd overlooked it on her first day inside the house.

Swirling the wine, she raised the glass against the sky's deepening reds and admired the color. She closed the patio door against the thickening wind. Inside, the house seemed darker than she remembered. Christina flicked on a lamp, disappointed when the light did little to drive back the shadows. Two shopping bags from her day at the Fair Haven Beach shops sat against the door where she'd dropped them after discovering the wine.

As she crossed from the living room into the entryway, a noise came from behind her. The moan of a floorboard. She spun back to the darkened living room, the sectional sofa dividing the floor from the large screen television on the wall. Old houses made scary sounds, she told herself. The wind clamored at the sliding glass door like it wanted to break through.

Snatching the bags, she climbed the staircase to the master bedroom. The floor-to-ceiling window offered a spectacular view of the water, and she contemplated reading a Thomas Harris novel while overlooking the ocean.

First, she determined to change into something more comfortable. Trading the dress shorts and tank for sweatpants and a baggy t-shirt, Christina padded barefoot into the hallway.

The noise came again. A dragged-out groan, like a monstrous beast creeping through the shadows.

This time she was sure it was a floorboard, not the fitful moan of a settling house. She stepped back from the rail. Heart thundering, she believed a prowler had broken into the rental. And her phone lay on the kitchen counter.

Quiet in the gloom, Christina backtracked to the bedroom and edged the door shut. A feeble hook-and-eye latch hung beside the door. Wincing when the lock rattled in her shaking fingers, she connected the pieces and stepped away. There had to be a phone in the room.

Except there wasn't. And the dark view through the window showed the next house several hundred yards down the beach.

She listened at the door. Ear pressed to the wood. Hands curled into fists and eyes clamped shut.

No sound came from downstairs. Had she overreacted to a random noise?

11

The clink of glass pulled her eyes open. Then the *glug-glug* of poured wine.

Yes, someone was inside the house. A hopeful thought occurred to Christina. Logan was downstairs. He sneaked inside to surprise her and partook in the gift he'd left on the counter.

Terror prevented Christina from calling her brother's name. Instead, she slid the windowpane up, cringing when the wood shrieked and gave her away.

The two-story plunge ended in a pile of sand and scrub grass. Too far to leap, but she'd take a broken leg over rape.

The screen remained the only barrier between Christina and freedom when the bedroom door imploded.

She shrieked as the flimsy lock burst off the jamb in a shower of splinters. It couldn't be Logan. Her brother wouldn't hurt her, would he?

The dark shadow filled the doorway. Christina shoved both hands through the screen and knocked it off its hinges. As she ripped the screen out of the frame and climbed onto the sill, his hands grasped her hair from behind and yanked.

Christina's head slammed against the hardwood. Her vision blurred as two hands clasped around her neck and lifted her off the floor as though she was a child's doll.

Legs kicking and flailing as he walked her across the room, Christina beat at the masked figure's head.

When he reached the wall, he smashed the back of her head against the plaster. Christina went limp. The room turned black.

Then the masked killer swept Christina into his arms. Almost lovingly.

The starlight caught the wicked gleam of his blade as he drew the edge across Christina's throat. Her body convulsed, and he hugged the dying woman, whispering in her ear that it was time to sleep, time to let go of the pain.

He stood over her, grinning.

Admiring the pooling blood.

Plastic wrapped around his shoes and up to his calves. He'd leave no identifying footprints, and the woman's DNA would be at the bottom of a dumpster after he discarded the plastic.

From inside his jacket, he removed a black sack and placed it over Christina Wolf's head.

"Come home, little one. Time to sleep."

CHAPTER THREE

The bright lights of the hospital stood in stark contrast to the night when the physician's assistant pulled the last stitch tight on Gardy's thigh.

Bell sat in the corner and waited for the assistant to clear the room. Gardy's legs dangled off the table like a child at his first doctor's exam.

"I hate stitches," he said, gritting his teeth when the man bandaged the wound and secured it with tape.

Bell leaned forward with her elbows on her knees.

"Be thankful the bullet grazed your thigh."

The talk of bullets and snipers won an unsettled look from the physician's assistant. He hurried out of the room as though he suddenly realized there was somewhere he needed to be.

"But I doubt the shooter aimed for your thigh," Bell said, tapping her keys against her leg. "For that matter, I'm unconvinced he targeted you."

"There you go trying to steal the spotlight. You said you saw the guy?"

"Hardly. I saw a shadow on the far side of the beach.

No way I could ID the bastard."

Gardy rubbed at his chin.

"So he fired from two hundred yards. Considering the strength of those wind gusts, I'd say he's a damn skilled shooter."

"The wind saved our lives. A light breeze, and the medical examiner would be pulling bullets out of our skulls."

"Nice thought."

The police had responded to the gunshots, and after learning the shooter struck one of their agents, the FBI arrived. With the FBI present, a police detective named Schroeder interviewed the two agents while Gardy awaited stitching. Neither Bell nor Gardy told the investigators anything useful.

"Funny," Bell said, meeting Gardy's eyes. "One second we're discussing a political assassination and Weber's involvement, and the next we're under fire."

"Hold up. *You* discussed Weber's involvement, I listened."

"And did you learn anything?"

"Only that losing a chunk off your thigh hurts like a son-of-a—"

"It's the same sniper, Gardy. The same killer who shot the congresswoman and tried to kill us in the alleyway."

"Must be more than one shooter," he said, picking at the tape. "Unless the guy you shot came back to haunt you."

A dark memory returned to Bell. The night she took down the God's Hand killer and rescued San Giovanni's daughter, a sniper shot at Bell and Logan Wolf on a

Virginia hillside. After she killed the sniper, she discovered a pendant around his neck. A pendant worn by special ops. When she directed the FBI to the sniper's coordinates, the body vanished.

Bell peeked down the hallway and closed the door.

"Former special ops soldiers don't come cheap, Gardy. You might not believe my conspiracy theories, but it's convenient the guy disappeared when the FBI investigated the hillside. Not a single bullet found, not even from my gun. How's that possible?"

"How is it possible Don Weber monitored our conversation and called a hit? Paranoia is getting the best of you."

"He's corrupt, and San Giovanni knew."

Gardy opened his mouth to argue and snapped it shut.

Bell's phone hummed inside her pocket. She entered her passcode and found a text from the BAU at the same time the message arrived on Gardy's phone.

Gardy squinted, holding the phone at arm's length as he read. His eyes widened.

"Impossible," Bell said.

The murder scene was still fresh, the body discovered inside a beach house in Fair Haven Beach, Florida, after an anonymous message tipped off the local police.

"That's Wolf's M.O. You still think he only murders male serial killers?"

Bell placed her hand over her mouth.

"Gardy, read the name of the victim."

"What's that have to do with…"

Gardy's mouth hung open. When he glanced at Bell, his eyes seemed to say the name had to be coincidental.

"Christina Wolf is a common name, Bell."

But he knew better. They both did.

"That's his sister's name. And I don't believe in coincidences."

As she read through the case briefing, Gardy eased himself off the table and hissed when his leg met the floor.

"So Wolf murdered his sister, same as he murdered his wife in 2013. I hope you realize Logan Wolf isn't some broken teddy bear you can take home and mend. He's a lunatic, Bell."

"Christina Wolf," Bell said, ignoring Gardy and reading the name aloud as if doing so would make sense of the situation. She swiped the phone over to her contacts list and phoned Harold, the BAU's technical analyst who possessed a knack for gathering background information on suspects and victims. "Harold, it's Bell. I need you to look up Christina Wolf's background and tell me if she's Logan Wolf's sister."

A pause.

"It's her," Harold said. "Christina Wolf, age forty. Younger sister of Logan Wolf. Divorced. Resides in Palm Beach, Florida."

Ending the call, Bell dropped her arm against her side. Had Logan Wolf lied to her and pulled the wool over her eyes? Or had the pressure of being on the run sent him over the edge and turned him against his last remaining family member?

"Harold confirmed it," Bell said, leaning against the wall. Her legs felt like rubber bands. "She's Logan's sister."

"Then it's time I did what I should have done months ago."

He shrugged into his jacket and reattached his holster.

"Oh, no you don't," Bell said, finding her sea legs. "You're injured. Until the FBI clears you for field work, you're on the sidelines."

"That never stopped you."

"The doctor hasn't released you from the hospital yet."

He glared impatiently at his watch.

"Fine. I'll stick around until the doctor springs me, but you're not going anywhere until I get word from Weber on my status."

"Too late, Gardy. The BAU booked my flight out of Dulles in four hours."

"What?" Gardy checked his phone and scrolled through his messages. "I didn't receive the flight notification."

"That's because Weber isn't sending you."

The truth struck Gardy, and he sank onto a chair and buried his face in his hands.

"This can't be happening. I'm this close to catching Wolf," Gardy said, pinching his fingers together for emphasis. "And they pull me from the case."

Glancing at the time, Bell felt her heartbeat quicken as a flutter of nervous energy moved through her stomach. It was always this way when the BAU called her to a new case and she needed to race against the clock. She did the math in her head—a quick stop at the apartment to grab her travel bag, which she kept packed for these situations, then she'd gas up the car and fight the DC traffic. If she hurried, she'd have time to eat a late dinner and still make her flight.

"You're not leaving me here, are you?"

"Sorry, Gardy. I'll lobby Weber on your behalf."

"That's what I'm afraid of."

Bell twirled the key ring around her finger and threw him a sympathetic glance over her shoulder.

"Get better, Gardy. I hope I see you in Florida."

CHAPTER FOUR

Too many questions. Not enough time.

During the trip home, Bell couldn't concentrate on the road. Logan Wolf dominated her mind. She'd believed him, though she never trusted the serial killer. Now she felt used, fooled, lied to. After almost causing an accident, she pulled into a gas station and closed her eyes. Around her, the world went about its business as though nothing unusual had occurred today. For Bell, the earth split open and swallowed her.

Her bag lay open on the passenger seat. Buried at the bottom in a hidden compartment, a burner phone hid from prying eyes. One of three Logan Wolf had given her. The fugitive often threw the prepaid phones away after one use, but since he trusted Bell, they often kept a phone for a week or more when they communicated frequently.

Though Bell had been aware Wolf had a sister, he never mentioned her. Bell had assumed he wanted to protect his sister and shield her from the madness surrounding his life. Why would he murder Christina?

After her head cleared, Bell pulled onto the interstate,

pushing the accelerator to make up for lost time. Traffic thinned along the Chesapeake Bay, but the late night traffic near DC would be a bear. Stars lit the sky from one horizon to the next. A strange orange glow grew out of the east. For a moment, she worried she'd fallen asleep at the gas station and lost track of time, but the dashboard clock read midnight.

As she turned down the coast road, a smoky scent reached her nose. Something was wrong. Anxious energy fueled her. Pushing harder on the gas, she navigated the black Nissan Rogue around hairpin curves, slowing only when she entered the residential area.

The shock of seeing her apartment complex on fire brought her to a screeching halt. Roadblocks prevented her from advancing, and a man directing traffic raised his hand at her and pointed in the opposite direction. He wanted her to turn around and leave.

She lowered the window and flashed her FBI badge.

"FBI. I need to get in there."

"Not tonight," the man said, turning his eyes toward the two firetrucks outside her apartment complex. "Nobody gets in."

Craning her neck around the man, Bell spied the unmarked black SUV at the back of the parking lot. Agent Flanagan. The FBI routinely positioned an agent at Bell's apartment complex, hoping to catch Logan Wolf. In the past, the fugitive had slipped around the FBI and entered Bell's apartment without drawing attention.

Bell waved to the volunteer and backed the Rogue down the road until she paralleled a flat patch of meadow. Swinging into the meadow, she locked the vehicle with the key fob and walked past the roadblock. The man warned her not to approach the fire, but he let her pass. It didn't hurt that she allowed her jacket to fall away from the Glock-22 on her hip.

From the back of the parking lot, she watched the flames snap along the roof of one apartment on the far right. The fire hadn't spread, but it would if the wind picked up. Behind her, a television news crew raced their van down the road only for the roadblocks to thwart them.

Flanagan, the hawk-nosed junior agent who trailed Bell during the Nicholas Winston serial killer case, leaned against the SUV, arms folded as though he expected her. She had questions for Flanagan. What was he doing in Blackwater, Virginia while Bell and Gardy pursued Winston? She assumed Weber had sent his pet-agent to spy on her. Bell painted on a smile as she strode up to the junior agent.

"How's Agent Gardy?" Flanagan asked.

"The bullet grazed his thigh. He's stitched up, but he'll be in pain for the next week. Did you see how the fire started?"

Flanagan extended his arm toward the ground-floor apartment three buildings over from hers.

"The fire started in the kitchen. A neighbor called it in before I noticed the smoke."

That was the O'Connor's apartment. The seniors were in Oregon visiting their daughter and had asked Bell to keep an eye on the place. How could the fire start in the kitchen with nobody home to cook?

Bell started forward, and Flanagan snatched her by the arm.

"You can't go inside."

"I'll be late for my flight. My bag is in my apartment."

But it was too late. The fire chief filed the neighbors out of her building where they wandered toward their cars like lost souls.

"Well, I guess I'm flying to Florida without a change of clothes," Bell said, placing her hands on her hips. "This should be interesting."

"New case, Agent Bell?"

"Weber didn't tell you?" She cocked an eyebrow, but Flanagan didn't take the bait. "You seem to know my every move. I've been meaning to ask why you drove to Blackwater."

"Blackwater? Oh, you mean the Winston murders."

"That's right."

"I'm sorry, Agent Bell, but you must be mistaken."

"Gardy and I saw you."

Flanagan shook his head and turned to watch the fire.

"I mean no offense, but I wasn't anywhere near Blackwater during the Winston case. Now if you don't mind, I'm heading back to the office since you're on the way to Dulles. Safe travels, Agent Bell."

Flanagan drove off and abandoned her in the parking lot. Liar. She didn't know what the junior agent was up to, but she'd keep eyes in the back of her head on future cases. The conspiracy theorist inside her believed Weber wanted dirt on Bell, a justification for firing her.

Directing hoses at the blaze, the firefighters appeared to have the blaze under control. They might clear her apartment for entry in the next several hours, but by then she'd be in Florida. Bell's neighbors asked her what she knew about the fire. She didn't have answers, only the usual platitudes to have faith. Things would be all right.

She walked back to the meadow, stepping with care

through a muddy area which tried to rip her shoes off. When she passed the roadblock, the volunteer firefighter manning the checkpoint waved her down.

"Hey, someone started creeping around your SUV while you were at the fire."

Bell stopped and squinted into the darkness. At the edge of the meadow, a shadow vanished behind a stand of trees.

"Did you see his face?"

"Too dark. I yelled, and he took off in that direction."

The volunteer gestured toward the trees where Bell spotted the shadow. She thanked the man and moved toward the Rogue with her gun drawn.

From her hip, she removed a flashlight and aimed it at her vehicle. No broken windshield, no random graffiti.

Her heart pounded in her ears as she swept the beam across the seats. Nobody hidden inside.

She was about to click the key fob when her instincts screamed something was wrong. Bell backed away and rounded the Rogue, studying the vehicle as she flicked the light over the doors. Then she bent down. An object caught her eye on the undercarriage. Too small for her to discern at night. The little box flashed a green light and turned dark again.

Dropping to her stomach, she swept the light over the undercarriage.

And saw the explosive.

CHAPTER FIVE

Bell's breath caught in her throat. She inched backward, watching the bomb as though a cobra coiled and hissed beneath the vehicle.

When she'd scrambled a safe distance from the Rogue, she jumped to her feet and put her hand over her heart. The man at the roadblock glared at her.

The Rogue rested a safe distance from the firefighters, but if the bomb exploded, debris would put the volunteer at risk. Breaking into a jog, she called Harold at the BAU and told him to send the bomb squad. By the time she ended the call, she stood at the curb, the volunteer taking a step away from the roadblock, sensing danger.

After she told him about the explosive, he contacted the fire chief. The man yelled orders over the radio.

"Are you certain you can't identify the man?" Bell asked.

"It's like I told you. It was too dark to get a good look at him, but now that you mention it, he looked under your vehicle."

Flanagan popped into her head.

"A black SUV drove out of the parking lot ten minutes ago. He must have passed your roadblock."

"I saw the SUV. Tinted windows, government plates."

"That's the one. The driver wasn't the man beside my vehicle, was he?"

The volunteer shook his head.

"No. I watched the SUV drive off. If he came back, I would have noticed."

The bomb squad spent a long time removing the explosive from underneath Bell's vehicle. She would miss her flight. Though the circumstances were beyond her control, Bell spent ten minutes on the phone with the angry deputy director who wanted to know why she wasn't in Florida.

"The next flight departs at nine o'clock. I expect you to be on it."

Weber hung up before she replied. The sun would be up soon, and she hadn't slept a wink. At least she was allowed to enter her apartment and grab her travel supplies.

The bomb squad leader, a tall man with a shaved head, glasses, and an ear piece attached to a wire, walked toward Bell as she pocketed her phone. She knew him as Cashman. The squad leader wore a dark blue uniform, making him difficult to see in the dark, and moved with purpose and efficiency as he crossed the meadow.

"You were lucky," Cashman said. "A radio transmitter controlled the explosive. He could have set it off at any time."

Bell's eyes swept the far end of the meadow. The bomber needed to stay close to fire the explosive. He fled after the bomb squad arrived.

"So starting the engine wouldn't have set it off."

"Nope. You attract a lot of bombers, Agent Bell?"

"I have a bad habit of pissing people off."

After the team cleared her Rogue, she drove to the apartment complex, nervous every time the tires hit a bump, worried another bomb lay hidden inside the vehicle. She slogged up the apartment steps, exhaustion smothering her anxiety as the sun peaked over the Atlantic. Inside, she gathered her belongings and grabbed snacks for the drive to Dulles. Her eyes swept the living room, suspicious, and stopped on the sliding glass door to the deck. From here she discerned the trench beside the ocean, the waves filling the excavation with sand. The trench where Gardy and Bell almost died.

The ride to the airport left her wondering about the bomb and the fire. Too coincidental. The past months' events made it obvious someone wanted her dead, and the attempts on her life had become a weekly occurrence.

As she swerved through highway traffic, her phone rang. Her mother's name appeared on the dash, and she accepted the call, worried her parents had more bad news. They planned to move to a retirement community in Arizona. Bell's research suggested the owner might be unscrupulous. Several retirees claimed the owner cheated them out of their savings.

"Were you in a fire?"

Tammy Bell's question took her daughter by surprise.

"How did you find out about the fire so fast?"

"Your father heard about it on the news. We were so worried."

"The fire didn't reach my building, Mom. I'm fine."

At least her mother hadn't learned about the bomb.

"That's so frightening. I hope nobody got hurt."

"Everyone made it out before the fire got out of hand, but one of my neighbors lost their belongings."

"Oh, that's horrible." Bell imagined her mother touching her heart and fanning her face, a habit she repeated whenever she encountered tragedy and loss. "Let us know if we can help. Your father and I have led a fortunate life."

"Yes, you tell me often. Is everything okay, Mom? It's only seven in the morning."

"Everything is wonderful. We keep hoping you'll stop by with Agent Wolf again. Your father can't stop talking about him."

Bell's stomach dropped as she remembered Logan Wolf paying a visit to her childhood home. She'd chalked the visit up to one of his mind games, but after his sister's slaughter, the memory sent a shiver down her spine.

"Agent Wolf is out of the country. We're not sure when he'll get back."

"A shame. Such a nice man. We were thinking of inviting him over to meet the—"

"Actually, Agent Wolf wants to transfer to another agency. We won't see much of him from now on."

Bell overheard her mother's disappointment as she told her husband the bad news.

"I almost forgot," Tammy Bell said, rummaging through the closet. "You received a package yesterday afternoon. No idea why they sent it to us, and there's no return address, but you'll need to pick it up when you have the time."

The Rogue swerved out of its lane and drew angry

horns from the other drivers.

"Don't touch the package."

"What do you mean? I'm holding the box right now."

Before Bell could stop her, Tammy Bell tore the box open. Heart surging into her throat, Bell prayed the next sound wouldn't be an explosion a split-second before the call cut off.

"Mom? Put the package down and wait for me."

"Well, isn't that odd? The box is empty."

"Empty? Why would anyone send me an empty box?"

"Wait a second. There's something under the paper."

"Are you listening to me?" Bell searched for an opening in the traffic glut. The next exit was less than a mile away. "Don't touch anything."

"It's a note. Strange. What does this mean?"

"What does the note say?"

"It reads, *Come home, little one. Time to sleep.*"

CHAPTER SIX

"I don't care if Weber hasn't cleared you for field work," Bell said, forcing her way through the crowd blocking her gate.

She'd sprinted from the TSA checkpoint to the gate, but the gate attendant hadn't boarded her row yet.

"You're the only person I trust. I want the note and box dusted for prints, hair fibers, anything that tells me who this person is."

"You believe it's the same guy who planted the explosive?" Gardy asked, raising his voice so she could hear him. He was at the office, waiting to meet with Weber.

"And the man who tried to take our heads off last night. Yes, Gardy."

"But why an empty box with a vague note stuffed in the bottom? If this guy wanted to send a message, he'd plant another explosive."

The gate attendant welcomed Bell's row to board. A brunette woman wearing too much makeup budged in front of Bell and clipped another passenger with the edge of her suitcase.

"Maybe he figured the delivery company would detect the explosive." Hearing Bell, the brunette woman swiveled her head around and edged away. "Or he's playing games with me. Hell, I don't know."

"Candice just rang my phone. Time to see Weber. I gotta go. Regardless of what he says, I'll pay your parents a visit as soon as I can."

"You're a lifesaver, Gardy."

Turbulence ruined the trip to Miami. Bell remembered Gardy's penchant for airsickness and thanked the heavens he wasn't on the flight. The elderly woman in the next seat moved to the back of the plane to sit with her family halfway through the trip, and Bell felt comfortable removing her iPad to page through the Fair Haven Beach crime scene photographs.

The slash across Christina Wolf's throat was clean and efficient, executed by a steady hand. This killer had experience. The ominous and familiar sack over the victim's head haunted Bell. She'd reviewed these macabre scenes too many times, and she never got used to them.

Next she paged forward to a recent photograph of Christina Wolf. The resemblance to Logan Wolf struck her. The firm set of the mouth, the high cheekbones, the inquisitiveness of the eyes. All eerily similar.

After she read through the police report, she put the iPad away and leaned back, closing her eyes. What sent Logan Wolf over the edge? If he'd wanted to murder his sister, why wait until now?

The smothering heat of summer had left Virginia for the year, but when Bell stepped through the sliding glass doors to pick up her rental car, she found where summer hid. The wall of sun and tropical maritime air blanketed

Bell as she slipped her sunglasses on and dodged the taxis and Uber drivers. She descended a short stairway to the rental lot and found her vehicle, a sporty red Kia with a long scratch across the hood. Placing her bag at her feet, Bell buckled under a wave of paranoia. A businessman talking on his phone eyed Bell curiously as she dropped to her stomach and checked the undercarriage. Clear, though the muffler was on its last legs.

The dashboard clock read noon as she fought highway traffic. Thank goodness for GPS, for she'd never visited the greater Miami area. The synthesized female voice directed her to the Fair Haven Beach police department. Checking her notes, Bell showed her badge at the front desk and asked for Detective Larrabee. As though she was poised at the door waiting for Bell, an African-American woman in a beige skirt suit and heels clicked across the operations area and held out her hand.

"Welcome to Fair Haven Beach, Agent Bell," Detective Larrabee said, her handshake firm. "Just you?"

"My partner is indisposed this afternoon, but I hope to have him with me by tomorrow."

"Good. Do you prefer to ride with me to the crime scene, or would you rather follow?"

Knowing by the time she finished the walk-through she'd need to hustle to the hotel and check in, Bell chose to follow Larrabee in her rental car. The trip took fifteen minutes.

Palms flanked the two-story beach house. A man and his beagle walked the otherwise empty beach as Larrabee pushed aside the yellow crime scene tape and unlocked the door.

"The owner has a house two miles south of here and

rents this place during the off season. Our vic paid for a week's stay." The cacophony the sea breeze caused vanished when Larrabee stepped into the foyer and closed the door. "We get our share of violence in the Miami area, but Fair Haven Beach is a vacation town. This time of year, the shops and restaurants close early, and everyone knows their neighbors by name."

Bell gave a non-committal nod and studied the layout. The foyer opened to a dated kitchen, an unusual layout for an older house. A bottle of Merlot rested on the counter beside an empty wine glass.

Slipping on a pair of gloves, Bell lifted the glass to the light and studied the edges.

"Did you test the glass for DNA?"

"We dusted for prints. You think the killer drank from the glass?"

"Just a hunch."

Beyond the kitchen, a living room held a sectional couch, television, and two end tables. The deck beyond the sliding glass door drew Bell's eye. Christina Wolf must have admired the ocean from the deck. God knew Bell would have.

"The killer entered through the deck door," Larrabee said, gesturing at the door. "He broke the latch and came inside, probably while the woman was away. We found two bags from the shopping plaza. No other signs of forced entry. The screen is off its hinges in the master bedroom. Apparently, she broke the screen trying to escape."

Larrabee led Bell up the stairs. The master bedroom lay at the end of the hallway, and one large window set on the eastern wall lent a view of the water. But the blood-soaked carpet held Bell's attention.

"We think the killer grabbed her at the window and pulled her back," the detective said, dropping to one knee beside the gore. "Then he killed her here. What we don't understand is why. Was this a random murder? Revenge?"

"Not vengeance. Not even rage."

"I thought most violent murders were rage-based."

"This murder is cold and calculated. No stab wounds, no strangulation. This almost looks like a contract killing." Bell swept her thumb across her throat. "Whoever our killer is, he kept his control. And he's done this before."

"A serial killer?"

"Perhaps."

After Larrabee finished the briefing, she sat in her car while Bell walked through the house. Since joining the BAU, Bell preferred to study the house alone, without the distraction of people offering opinions and breaking her concentration.

She began at the patio door. Latches on sliding glass doors are notoriously easy to jostle open. A smart killer would begin here, and Logan Wolf was the most intelligent murderer she'd studied. From the deck, he could have watched Christina. Fantasized the murder before he acted.

Sand speckled the deck, not unusual for a patio overlooking the beach. The door opened to the living room. No hiding places here, but a closet off the foyer intrigued Bell. She pictured Christina at the counter opening the bottle of wine. She might have heard the ceiling groan and gone upstairs to investigate.

No, that didn't feel right.

Sticking to the shadows bleeding down from the walls, following the arc the killer likely would have taken, Bell stepped through the kitchen and pulled the closet door open. More sand dotted the bare wood floor. Backtracking through the living room, she discovered sand in the shadows. The cleanliness of the downstairs suggested the owner tidied up after coming inside and wouldn't leave a speck of sand. Yes, the killer took this path and hid inside the closet.

After stepping into the closet, Bell stood in darkness. Even with the door closed, she peered through the sliver-opening between the door and jamb. She pictured Christina pouring wine at the counter, taking a sip and carrying the glass of Merlot out to the deck. For many serial killers, a voyeuristic viewing of the target offered sexual gratification. He might have fantasized. Christina Wolf was a pretty woman who kept herself in shape.

Except Logan Wolf wouldn't fantasize about his sister.

He might have gifted Christina the Merlot. That sounded like Wolf. But little else fit beyond the precise sweep of the blade against Christina's neck.

Now she pictured Wolf's sister on the deck, one arm leaned against the rail as she took in the ocean view. A perfect time for the killer to emerge from the closet and climb the stairs toward the bedrooms. Christina could have turned around and looked past the deck door, the killer invisible to her inside the dark living room. He stared at her, Bell thought. The thrill of knowing she was so close yet couldn't see him.

She replayed the murder scene in her head upstairs. Struggled to imagine Wolf in the killer's role. Something didn't fit.

She took pictures of the house on her way out. After suggesting Larrabee dust for prints inside the closet, she left for the hotel.

Wolf didn't murder his sister.

CHAPTER SEVEN

From the parking garage rooftop across the street, he studies the photograph and compares it to the beautiful woman at the hotel check-in desk. Scarlett Bell, an agent with the FBI.

She's alone. Vulnerable.

The man behind the desk hands her the key card, and she lifts the travel bag at her feet. Through the binoculars, he follows her to the corner room on the second floor, 215. The Florida sun scorches the pavement, but he sticks to the cool shadows and slides along the concrete wall until he stands even with her room.

Agent Bell fumbles the key card and kneels to pick it up, and he glimpses bare thigh when her skirt runs up. His heart hammers when she suddenly spins and looks directly at him. Yes, she senses him. Can feel him in the shadows the way a grasshopper does the trapdoor spider.

He edges back, ensures the darkness cloaks his presence. After a tense moment, she opens the door and disappears inside.

The man smiles. He's butchered dozens, though never

had he killed for money. For fifteen years, he's traveled the back roads of the United States, stealing the unprotected from their families and claiming them as his own. He's careful. Methodical. And he doesn't make mistakes, which is why he never attracted attention. No buried bodies for a weekend warrior geologist to uncover, no manifestos sent to the nation's largest newspapers. His trophies travel with him.

He touches the black van's sliding door. The four sealed barrels stand on the other side of the door. His butterfly collection.

No mistakes. He's a ghost.

Which makes him wonder how the FBI man wearing the blue suit, ear piece, and sunglasses found him in 2013. The government knew he was a murderer, though he doubted the FBI appreciated how many lives ended at his hands. But they didn't arrest him. They wished to hire him.

On a hot evening in July of 2013, he crept inside the residence of Logan and Renee Wolf. His instructions were clear—slaughter the woman without leaving a trace of his presence and make the murder appear ritualistic. Interesting. He didn't get off on the ritualistic bullshit. Taking a life and keeping it for his own satisfied him. The 2013 murder left him cold and detached. Though he enjoyed slitting the woman's throat, stuffing her head into a black bag felt forced, contrived.

Now the FBI had found him again. He felt certain they would arrest him this time, but the new FBI agent, a thin, young man with a hawk nose, handed him three photographs. Targets. If he murdered all three, the FBI wouldn't pursue him. They'd continue to pretend he didn't exist. A fair deal, though temptation urged him to gut the

FBI agent for threatening him.

He followed the first woman for a week before she rented the vacation home along the ocean. The attraction he felt for her mystified him. There was something dangerous about her, something clandestine, as though she clung to a dark secret. He senses she is related to the woman they asked him to eliminate in 2013. Renee Wolf.

He had his own methodologies for killing beautiful women, but the agent insisted he slit the woman's throat and place a bag over her head as he'd done in 2013. He doesn't understand why. Doesn't care. Taking a life excites him and leaves him sleepless for days, and last night he relived the murder as he stared up at the ceiling in his van, the barrels beside him, the scents of metal, death, and rust stewing.

Slipping the photograph of Agent Bell into the envelope, he studies the last picture. A man. He never butchered a man before. Not for pleasure, anyway.

In the cool gloom of the garage, he unlocks the door and slides the pictures under the driver seat. Then the man pockets the keys and crosses the busy thoroughfare, heedless of the Corvette that screeches to a halt and assails him with a horn. He enters the main lobby and passes the front desk without generating interest. The hallway is dark. Voices travel from behind locked doors, unaware death passes on silent footsteps. Eschewing the elevator, he takes the stairs at the end of the corridor. Concrete and echoes.

One flight up, he edges the door open and stands outside room 215. He touches the door and imagines Agent Bell on the other side, placing her hand against the barrier to mirror his. Like lost soul mates.

He will kill her tomorrow.

The Redeemer

CHAPTER EIGHT

Bell shot awake. Someone was outside the door.

Grabbing her holster off the bed, she placed her eye against the peephole. The balcony lay empty. Her nerves had gotten the better of her again.

An hour remained before she briefed the Fair Haven Beach PD, and she had no idea what to say. The BAU asserted Logan Wolf murdered his sister. She wouldn't lie to a room of law enforcement officers.

A message arrived from Gardy. Her partner left a half-hour ago and would be in Bealton soon. Had they made the right decision by not involving the FBI at her parents' house? To the untrained eye, the note looked like a practical joke. But Bell sensed a more ominous intent.

She showered and changed, and as she grabbed her phone off the nightstand, it rang. Except it didn't. It took her several confused seconds before she realized the ringing came from her bag. Wolf's burner phone.

Bell tossed the bag's contents across the bed and snatched the phone before it stopped ringing.

"Wolf?"

She waited for the serial killer's eerie sing-song voice. When he spoke, he sounded different. Shattered. Furious.

"You were wrong, Scarlett. I warned you not to fail me."

Bell sat on the edge of the bed.

"The profile of Renee's killer is correct. Now, tell me where you were last night."

Laughter.

"Am I a suspect, dear Scarlett? Do you think I…" His voice broke. Wolf lowered the phone against his chest and composed himself. "Since the night that butcher stole Renee, I've tracked this killer. You told me he didn't exist, that someone murdered my wife and set me up. But now this. My only remaining family. Gone because I believed you."

"I just returned from studying the murder scene, but I guess you already knew."

"To prove I killed Christina?"

Bell held her response, searching for the right words.

"To prove to myself you didn't."

"I could have saved you the effort."

"But you were there." Quiet followed. "The bottle of Merlot. That's something you would do."

His silence spoke volumes.

"Yes, I left the bottle. Christina always appreciated a fine wine, and I wanted to surprise her and give her happiness. She deserved it after all she'd gone through. But I didn't murder my sister. I wouldn't harm a hair on her head."

"This is a problem, Wolf. Your DNA is inside the house. If the CSI crew found anything to implicate you, there's nothing I can do."

"I was careful. I never touched the bottle without gloves. But I could have protected Christina had I any idea she was in danger."

Bell parted the curtain and looked down upon the hotel grounds. A pool with two children swimming, the father sipping a tropical drink. Palms swaying. A rundown hotel next door with plenty of dark shadows behind its walls.

"Are you in Fair Haven Beach, Wolf?"

"What if I am, Scarlett?"

"Leave. Someone set a trap for you. Don't you see?"

"If you think I'll leave with the man who killed Renee and Christina so close, you're the one who's insane."

"This man didn't kill Renee. That was a professional hit."

"Yes, yes. You keep repeating yourself, but you're wrong. I overestimated your profiling ability, I fear. You've led me to dead ends one too many times. It pains me to blame you, dear Scarlett, but you're responsible for Christina's death. And now you must pay. An eye for an eye."

The call ended. Bell stared at the phone as it trembled in her hand. She dropped it to the bed as though it morphed into a scorpion.

Back at the window, she peeked between the curtains. She opened the door and swept her gaze along the street. A college age girl rode past on a bicycle. Cars motored from one red light to the next.

Her eyes stopped on the three-level parking garage across the street. A black van with tinted windows pulled out of the garage and turned the corner, speeding past the building before she got a look at the license plate.

Then she spied the dark figure at the end of the block. Watching her from behind a stand of palms.

Logan Wolf.

CHAPTER NINE

"You're sure you can't stay for dinner?"

Gardy didn't want to impose on Tammy Bell, and besides, he'd lied to Weber and claimed he needed to see his doctor for a second opinion on his leg. The deputy director would ask questions if Gardy lingered in Bealton.

Though Mrs Bell had placed her fingers all over the box and note, Gardy wore gloves as he searched for evidence to identify the sender. He found nothing. Whoever sent the box, he was experienced and careful.

Come home, little one. Time to sleep.

Gardy didn't understand the meaning of the message. Mind games from the same man who placed the explosive under Bell's vehicle?

"Smells great, Mrs Bell, but they need me back at work."

"You're limping, Agent Gardy."

"It's nothing. I pulled a muscle at the gym. I guess my back squat isn't what it used to be."

The level look she gave Gardy told him she wasn't buying it.

"Well, you'd think the FBI would grant you time to heal before tossing you into the field. Speaking of which, Scarlett threw a fit over this little box. I worry she's under too much stress. She's not thinking straight."

"I'll keep an eye on her, Mrs Bell."

"I know you will, Agent Gardy. You're a good man. You'd make a fine husband someday, and I've tried to convince Scarlett to settle down—"

"I need to get back to Quantico," Gardy said, his cheeks blooming.

He tossed the box in the trunk and pondered the note's meaning while he followed Bealton's roads back to the highway. The little town held ghosts. Every street corner reminded him of the God's Hand killer and Logan Wolf, and he wondered how different Bell's life would have been had she grown up elsewhere.

His unease grew. Something about Bell's trip to Florida didn't sit right in his stomach. Why hadn't Weber sent another agent in Gardy's place? Between the multiple attempts on their lives, neither Bell nor Gardy should have been in the field.

He popped four ibuprofen in the parking lot. The stitches stretched and burned when he climbed out of his van, the wound tightening after the long drive. Under the late day sun, it was impossible to see beyond the windows, but Gardy felt Weber watching him as he climbed the steps. Gardy did his best not to limp.

Candice, Weber's administrative assistant, blew into Gardy's office the moment he sat down.

"Deputy Director Weber wishes to see you. Now."

Gardy sighed and straightened the stack of paperwork Candice had left him and slid it to the corner.

He felt tempted to sweep the mess into the garbage can.

The wound screamed at him, and he stood in the doorway and took a composing breath as he willed the pain away. Then he continued down the hallway to Weber's office, nodding at passing agents as if he didn't have a worry in the world.

Weber didn't look up when Gardy knocked, only motioned toward a chair as he jotted information on a form.

"How's the leg, Agent Gardy?"

"Better."

"Not good enough for field work. Let it heal and you'll be back in no time."

"Sir, if I may. Agent Bell is alone at Fair Haven Beach. There's no reason I can't catch the next flight to Miami and be there to watch her back."

"You're not fit to work, and Agent Bell is a big girl. She can handle a murder case on her own."

"Two attempts on her life in the last twenty-four hours. Why is she even allowed in the field?"

Weber groaned and leaned his elbows on his desk. After rubbing his eyes, he tapped his pen on the desk.

"Perhaps I was too hasty sending Agent Bell to Florida alone. You understand my desire to act before Logan Wolf pulls another vanishing act."

"You're certain Wolf is in Florida?"

"That can't be a serious question. The killer's M.O. matches Wolf's, and a traffic camera in Fair Haven Beach caught a man who resembled Wolf two hours before the murder."

As much as Gardy wanted to implicate Logan Wolf, Weber's shifting eyes belied him.

"All the more reason to send backup to Florida."

"Agreed. I'll send Agent Flanagan."

"Flanagan?" Gardy sat forward and squinted at Weber. "He's a junior agent. You can't send him to a case this big."

"Agent Flanagan has proved himself and won't be a junior agent for long. You didn't protest when I put Flanagan on duty to watch Agent Bell's apartment, so why complain now?"

"That's different."

"How so? If Logan Wolf appeared, Agent Flanagan would have apprehended him."

Gardy bit his lip. Weber had sent Flanagan to spy on them at Blackwater Lake, and he didn't trust the junior agent. Time for Plan B.

"You're right. Bell can handle the case on her own. With my injury, Agent Flanagan should slide into my role. I have paperwork to catch up on, anyhow."

"That's a sudden change of heart."

"Now that I think about it, Deputy Director Weber, my leg is bothering me. All this sitting around isn't good for the healing process. I'll take you up on your offer and accept the sick leave."

Weber narrowed his eyes.

"Strange the pain increased so suddenly."

"I should take a week off. Rest up and make sure the wound heals. I don't want the injury to linger for months because I rushed back into service."

"All right, Agent Gardy. I'll have Candice give you the paperwork."

Gardy pushed up from his chair, limping to play up the pain.

"I better not find out you flew to Florida, Agent

Gardy. Lying about an injury and claiming sick leave could mean your job."

Gardy grabbed his keys and took the elevator down to the ground floor. Throwing looks over his shoulder, he ensured nobody followed as he unlocked his van and pulled himself into the driver seat. As he pointed the vehicle toward the DC suburbs, he dialed Bell. She sounded harried when she answered.

"Someone's following me, Gardy."

At that moment, he checked his mirror and noticed a black SUV trailing him, staying several car lengths back.

"That makes two of us. You get a look at the guy?"

"I've seen Logan Wolf enough times to recognize him."

"Wolf is there? I figured he'd flee by now."

Gardy's pulse quickened. Bell without backup and Logan Wolf stalking her. He needed to get to Florida.

"Wolf didn't kill Christina, Gardy. I know you think he murdered his sister and wife, but it doesn't add up."

"So someone else murdered Christina Wolf? How many serial killers can one village hold?"

"Wolf blames me, but I'm sure the profile I gave him is correct. And what do you mean, someone is following you?"

"Maybe I caught your conspiracy flu," Gardy said, adjusting the mirror. "But there's a black SUV seven cars behind me. He's been there since I hit the interstate."

"Be careful, Gardy. You don't know if it's the sniper."

"Well, he can't line up a shot while driving seventy outside of DC. And I doubt TSA will let him board with a rifle."

"Don't tell me Weber allowed you to fly to Florida."

"Of course not. I'm injured and can't do my job. It's best for everyone I take a week of sick leave."

Bell snickered.

"Nicely played."

Gardy swerved into the passing lane and shot past a pickup truck. A moment later, the black SUV executed a pass and kept pace.

"I thought so, but Weber is on to me. Which explains my tail. But I'm stopping at the San Giovanni estate before I beg, borrow, or steal a ticket at the airport."

"The estate? Why are you stopping there?"

"Something you said. San Giovanni found dirt on a politician but didn't bring it to the committee."

"How would the mother know?"

"She might not, but I bet the mother remembers where San Giovanni kept her files."

He told Bell he hadn't identified the box's sender in Bealton, but he left out Tammy Bell suggesting he'd make a fine husband for Scarlett. Gardy couldn't deny his heart beat faster when Bell entered the room, but there was no future in pursuing a fellow agent, especially one who didn't show the slightest interest in him.

Gardy frowned.

"I don't get it. A serial killer murders Christina Wolf after a sniper shoots at us and someone places a bomb under your vehicle."

"The events are related, Gardy. I haven't connected the dots, but I will."

When Gardy took the exit ramp, the mysterious SUV disappeared.

CHAPTER TEN

Bell didn't recall the last time she felt this lost on a case.

She kept her briefing vague for the Fair Haven Beach PD, and by the time she finished, she hadn't conveyed new knowledge. Now she bristled under the stare of Detective Larrabee.

Seated behind her desk and irritably rocking in her chair, Larrabee ordered Bell to close her office door.

"You're holding out on me, Agent Bell."

"Why do you say that?"

"You danced around that briefing, and you don't buy half the theories you put forth."

Beneath the desk, Bell dug her nails into her thighs. She couldn't lie to Larrabee, nor could she tell her the truth. Before Bell opened her mouth to reply, Larrabee reached inside her desk and slid a photograph in front of Bell. A picture of Logan Wolf.

"Your own people say this man murdered Christina Wolf. Turns out he's my vic's brother, and if that isn't enough, he's a fugitive and the most renown serial killer in the United States. But you don't believe he did it."

"Did someone at the FBI call you?"

"I have my sources. Answer the question."

Bell picked up the picture and studied it. Wolf was younger then, an agent with the BAU. A flicker of hope still burned in those dark chasms for eyes. She could continue to lie to Larrabee, but it wasn't worth the trouble. By this time next week, she'd either be dead or out of a job.

"Yes, Logan Wolf is the victim's brother, but he didn't kill her."

"Explain your reasoning, Agent Bell, and it better be good."

Larrabee's face remained unreadable as Bell detailed Wolf's background and her theories about the serial killer. Why he killed. Her belief he never murdered his wife. It occurred to Bell Larrabee was the first person besides Gardy she'd confided in about Wolf's innocence in 2013. When Bell finished, Larrabee turned a pen over and over on the desk, eyes unblinking.

"Now that's the briefing I expected when I requested FBI assistance. If you'd given me anything half that good, we'd already have the perpetrator behind bars."

"I don't understand the murder, Detective."

Larrabee rocked back in her chair and set her heel on a drawer.

"What's the confusion?"

"This serial killer struck without emotion. The cut across Christina Wolf's throat is too perfect, too precise. It more resembles a contract hit than the act of a deranged murderer. And yet the unknown subject displayed characteristics of typical serial killers."

"Such as?"

"He didn't storm inside at the first opportunity and execute Christina Wolf. Instead, he stalked her. Watched her from the closet, maybe sipped from the wine bottle." Bell shook her head. "It's as if he switched midstream from lunacy to a paint-by-numbers murder."

"It's difficult for me to accept the killer isn't Logan Wolf when the method of killing matches his."

"This sounds crazy, Detective, but the killer wanted us to think Wolf murdered his sister."

The theory hung in the air as silence blanketed the room. Bell expected Larrabee to snatch her phone and dial the BAU to complain about the rogue field agent sitting across from her. Instead, she examined Bell the way she might an interesting piece of art she hadn't figured out.

"Two serial killers in Fair Haven Beach. I hope you're wrong, Agent Bell."

An Internet search returned five liquor stores in the village. One stuck out to Bell. D'Angelo's catered to discerning connoisseurs, people who appreciated fine wines. On her way to D'Angelo's, Bell phoned her mother and suggested her parents visit Helen, their friend in Fredericksburg. Tammy Bell listed all the reasons they shouldn't go, but Bell persisted until she agreed. Good. One less thing to worry about in case another package arrived.

The shopkeeper, an Italian man with black, slicked hair and a pencil-thin mustache, recognized Logan Wolf from the picture Bell showed him.

"An interesting man," the shopkeeper said, smiling. "And he knows his wines. He purchased our finest bottle of Merlot, paid with large bills, and told me to keep the change. It was a generous tip."

He estimated Wolf visited around one o'clock. Wolf's sister hadn't taken the house keys from the realtor until noon, so that meant Wolf already knew her plans. He must have followed her for days.

Calling up a map on her phone, Bell studied the terrain around the beach house. Like Miami, Fair Haven Beach was pancake-flat along the coast. Palms blocked the view from the nearest neighborhood. Nowhere to stake out the beach house without drawing attention.

Bell stopped at a surf shop three blocks from the ocean and purchased a beach hat, a new pair of sunglasses, a lounge chair, and a swim dress. To complete the disguise, she plucked a Dan Brown paperback off the counter. The teen boy working the desk took one look at Bell and agreed when she asked to use the changing room.

Bell cursed herself for not remembering sunscreen as she danced over the hot sand. The beach was empty except for a fisherman casting a line a hundred yards down the coast. Keeping the beach house in view, she walked until the two-story home appeared toy-like. Then she set her chair where the tide clawed at the sand. She raised her binoculars.

Perfect. She had a clear view of the deck door and the flapping crime scene tape. If the killer returned to relive the crime, she'd see.

A man approached from behind. Alone.

Bell opened the book and hid the binoculars inside her bag. She heard him stomp through the shallows, the gulls scattering.

False alarm. A woman shouted from further up the beach, and the man, obviously her husband, rushed to meet her.

The day grew late. Shadows lengthened and played tricks on Bell, fooling her into believing the killer had returned to the beach house.

At six o'clock, she began to feel foolish. She'd lose the sun soon, and the burn across her shoulders would leave her wishing for a sweatshirt.

But as she lowered the binoculars, a man rounded the beach house and ducked beneath the deck.

CHAPTER ELEVEN

How can a mansion be a tomb?

That question rolled around in Gardy's mind as he walked the desolate halls of the San Giovanni estate. Footsteps announced Joelle's presence upstairs, but San Giovanni's daughter hid inside her room and didn't show her face. Pots clanged in the kitchen as the cook prepared dinner, the echoes lonely.

The grandmother, Alessia San Giovanni, looked strikingly similar to her daughter, though the lines in her face dug deeper than when Gardy last saw her a month ago. She wore a black dinner dress to match the pitch of her hair, and her heels tapped the glistening floor as she led Gardy past the dining room and kitchen toward the study.

"Lana kept a laptop in her bedroom, but she did most of her work in the study," Alessia said, hands clasped at her waist.

"As long as you understand this isn't an official visit," said Gardy, his eyes drawn to the impressionist paintings lining the corridor. "Technically, I shouldn't be here."

Alessia glanced at him from the corner of her eye.

"Agent Gardy, you and Agent Bell are the only people Lana trusted in her final days, so I wouldn't let anyone near her computer but you. I can't promise you'll find anything useful. Lana remained secretive, even with her family, but she shared her access codes with me."

The study was the mansion's most impressive room. Stretching two stories along the back of the house, the glass ceiling offered unobstructed views of the sky. Long windows took up most of the back wall. One could lounge on the sofa and watch the sun rise.

It took a minute for the computer to reboot, then Alessia slipped a note card of passwords in front of Gardy.

"I'll leave you to it, Agent Gardy. Find my daughter's killer."

Alessia shut the door, and Gardy felt tiny inside the cavernous room. He began his search, stepping through file folders and sub-folders, until he discovered the work files for the corruption task force. From his pocket, he removed a list of cases the task force took public. Gardy checked off each case until he found a file that didn't link to any known cases.

Ewing.

Senator Chet Ewing, Gardy thought to himself as he double-clicked the file. Random characters filled the window, eliciting a curse from Gardy. San Giovanni had encrypted the file. This would take longer than expected. Checking the time, he realized he only had ninety minutes to drive to Dulles and catch his flight to Florida.

"What did you have on Ewing?" Gardy muttered, picking up the phone.

He called Harold's direct line at the BAU, relieved the technical analyst hadn't left for the day.

"I'm sending you a file, Harold. How fast can you decrypt a document?"

"Depends on the encryption strength," said Harold, calling up a terminal window on his workstation. "Uh, aren't you on sick leave?"

"As far as Weber knows."

"My lips are sealed."

"Like Belinda Carlisle."

"Who?"

"Never mind, just break the code before I miss my flight."

Harold typed away at his keyboard.

"Going somewhere, Agent Gardy?"

"I'm thinking someplace warm and tropical."

Harold issued a nervous snicker. The technical analyst knew Weber had eyes everywhere inside the BAU.

"Cracked it. Give me a harder challenge next time."

"You're a genius, Harold."

"I trust you'll remember who stuck their neck out for you come Christmas. The decrypted file is headed your way."

Harold's email popped up, and Gardy sent the file to his iPad.

"I'm heading to Dulles now. Thanks a million, Harold."

The list of cancellations didn't affect Gardy's flight to Miami, but a delay at the TSA checkpoint left him hobbling for the gate before the plane took off. He sent Bell a message and promised details on the Ewing file, but she didn't answer.

Night spread toward the runway as the flight crew prepared for takeoff. The cabin lights shut off, and the interior became dark. When the plane climbed to cruising altitude, Gardy removed the iPad from his seat compartment and called up the file.

Halfway through the document, he feared for Bell's life.

CHAPTER TWELVE

Gun in hand, Bell crept along the tall grass and dunes. She'd read Gardy's message and knew San Giovanni had dirt on Senator Ewing. It must have been big since the information got San Giovanni murdered. But why was Bell in the cross-hairs?

The pitched roof of the beach house jutted above the sand. The rest of the home hid from her sight. Digging the phone out of her pocket, she dialed Larrabee. The detective would be there in fifteen minutes.

But Bell didn't have fifteen minutes. Full dark raced across the ocean and cloaked the intruder. He might be anywhere in the dark. Even right behind her.

She ducked low and ran to the palms, cursing the narrow trunks that did little to conceal her presence as she placed her back against a tree. Then she spun off the tree and sprinted to the wall, keeping her head below the first-floor windows.

When she rounded the house, she squinted her eyes, trying to make out the shadows beneath the deck. Impossible to see. The gun trembled in her hand as she slid along the wall and edged closer to the stairs. Close enough to make out shapes, she discerned footprints beneath the deck.

One hand on the rail, Bell pulled herself onto the deck and stood with her back to the wall. From here, she could see the snapped crime scene tape and the unlocked latch to the sliding glass door. On a silent count of three, Bell reached out and slid the door open, thankful it whispered along the grooves. She spun inside the dark confines.

The hand reached out of the shadows and gripped her by the throat. His other hand knocked the Glock from her hand and covered her mouth. She couldn't see the man's face, only his silhouette as he shoved her against the wall. She brought her elbow against his arm, but he was too strong. As she squirmed along the wall, a glint of moonlight caught Logan Wolf's face.

"Wolf, let go."

"Why should I, Scarlett? Because of you I have no family."

Bell swung her head forward and knocked it against his. His eyes crossed, and his hand sprang off her neck. She sucked air into her lungs, but he dropped down and snagged her gun. Now he took a step backward and aimed the Glock at her chest.

"I knew you'd come," he said, shifting to stand between Bell and the deck door. "You're as predictable as a sunrise. You'll go to your grave believing I murdered Christina and came back to…what is it you profilers call it? …relive the crime."

"No. You didn't kill your sister. But you're walking into a trap, Wolf."

"It appears I laid the trap for you, dear Scarlett."

"Someone wants us dead, Gardy included. It got me thinking about the night the killer took Renee's life."

"Be careful. You're walking a razor's edge mentioning her name."

"Put the gun down, and let's talk this through."

"Not a chance."

Bell rolled her neck. Phantom fingers curled around her throat.

"The sniper who shot at us on the hill, the man who tried to kill Gardy and me, and Congresswoman San Giovanni's assassin. They're all interconnected, and you're at the center."

"A serial killer took my wife, just as he murdered Christina. He's still in the village, Scarlett. I can sense him. And before I leave this little village, I'll feed him his heart."

A sound came from outside. Someone running through the sand.

"We have a visitor," Wolf said, turning his attention toward the windows.

"I called for backup. If I were you, I'd put the gun down and vanish. I doubt Detective Larrabee came alone."

A second set of footsteps circled the house.

"You buy these conspiracy theories. I see it in your eyes. Interesting."

"Think back, Wolf. Did you investigate Senator Ewing?" Stunned, Wolf glared at Bell. The corner of his mouth twitched. "Because San Giovanni started a file on Ewing, and a month later, a sniper put a bullet in her head."

Wolf shook his head.

"No, it can't be. A serial killer murdered Renee."

"That's what he wants you to believe. Tell me what

you knew about Ewing."

Wolf flung the sliding glass door open and escaped into the night a split-second before the police burst into the house.

"Freeze, police!"

"Don't shoot, Larrabee. It's Agent Bell."

Bell raised her hands. The lights flicked on, blinding her. Larrabee, dressed as Bell had last seen the detective, rushed into the room beside a male officer a head taller than her.

Bell walked to the staircase and craned her head toward the landing, a diversion to pull Larrabee away from the deck. Though Wolf threatened her, Bell felt an undefinable need to protect him. He was just as much a victim as Renee and Christina.

"Was the killer here?" Larrabee asked, drawing her gun.

"A man broke inside," Bell said, nodding at the torn police tape flapping in the wind. "He must have heard me, because he jumped off the deck and ran toward the neighborhood before I could cut him off."

"I want the CSI team back," Larrabee barked at her partner. "Have them dust the door for prints and go over the downstairs with a fine-tooth comb. Find out who was in this house tonight."

Wolf wore gloves, but Bell worried he'd left a trace of DNA evidence behind.

"The team is on their way," the officer said.

"Thanks, Vargus. Agent Bell, meet Officer Luke Vargus."

Vargus tipped his cap. Bell touched her neck, drawing Larrabee's attention.

"You okay?" Larrabee asked Bell.

"Yeah, I slept wrong on the plane."

Larrabee nodded without taking her eyes off Bell. With her partner on the phone, Larrabee inched closer, her hand brushing the hair off Bell's face.

"It looks like someone grabbed you. Your neck is red."

"I keep rubbing at the pain, trying to loosen it up."

"Stop by my car on the way out. I keep aspirin in the glove compartment."

Bell waited with Larrabee and described the approximate size and age of the intruder. A half-hour later, the CSI team arrived.

As the crew went to work, Bell checked her phone. No news from Gardy.

Did Senator Ewing order the hit on San Giovanni?

CHAPTER THIRTEEN

The knock on the hotel room door pulled Bell out of sleep. Night butted against the window. Too early for housekeeping.

Bell crept to the peephole and exhaled at the sight of Gardy, her exhausted partner leaning against the door frame.

She unlatched the bolt and let him wander inside, a carry-on bag tossed over his shoulder.

"What time is it?" Bell asked, squinting when she flipped the light on.

Her nightshirt rode up her hips, and she tugged it down as he pulled his eyes to the wall.

"It's too late to be awake." He tossed the bag in the corner and slumped into the lounge chair in the corner. "Sorry. No vacancies in the village. Do you mind if I crash?"

"No, no. You can stay. It means a lot that you came."

He rubbed his eyes and yawned.

"First things, first. You'll want to see this file."

"Hold on, Gardy. I need to wake up."

Bell pulled a half-full soda bottle from the refrigerator and took a swig while Gardy loaded the Ewing file. She raised a finger and disappeared into the bathroom. Closing the door, she scowled at the mess of hair atop her head and ran a brush through the knots. Testing her breath against her palm, she grabbed her toothbrush and scoured the stench out of her mouth.

By the time she finished, her head cleared of the grogginess. She leaned over Gardy's shoulder and began reading.

After a minute, she sat on the corner of the bed and dropped her face into her hands.

"This can't be true. If it is, Ewing is—"

"A cold-blooded killer." Gardy scrolled to the middle of the document. "San Giovanni asserts Senator Klein's car crash wasn't an accident."

Twelve years ago, Senator Klein held an eight-point advantage in the polls over Ewing before his car shot off the interstate during a rain storm and ended up at the bottom of the Potomac.

"You didn't read all the way to the bottom," Gardy said, handing Bell the tablet.

Gardy spun the chair toward Bell, who skimmed through the congresswoman's findings. Her eyes froze over the last paragraph.

Against the orders of his superiors, one FBI agent investigated Klein's death and suspected foul play. A BAU agent named Logan Wolf.

The new knowledge hung like a sword and kept them silent. When they finally debated the findings, neither could keep their eyes open.

Bell wasn't certain when she fell asleep. She recalled

thrashing beneath the covers, the implications of the secret document haunting her every time she closed her eyes. Now the sun beamed through the windows. Gardy lay curled under a sliver of blanket at the foot of the bed.

Bell sighed and folded the covers over him. He made a contented groan and pulled the sheet over his face.

The shower spray steamed the bathroom. Bell leaned one arm against the wall as the water cascaded over her head. According to San Giovanni's findings, Ewing built a network of mercenaries and special ops soldiers. She hadn't uncovered the money trail before she died.

Bell toweled her hair dry, adrenaline keeping her upright when her body wanted to sleep another eight hours. After she dressed, she found Gardy awake and waiting for her on the chair.

His cheeks colored when she turned on the light.

"I don't remember crawling into your bed. That was terrible of me."

"If anyone should have the bed, it's you. That chair must be murder on your leg."

"Pretty damn inappropriate, though."

"Gardy, I trust you," Bell said, wondering what might have happened had she woken before dawn and found Gardy sleeping beside her.

"Anyway, it won't happen again." Bell flicked him with the towel. "What was that for?"

"You snore."

"I don't."

"Really now? You sound like a cow with a tuba stuck up its—"

"Fine. Can we get breakfast and figure out how to handle this Ewing situation?"

"There's a cafe down the block. I hope you brought something besides your work clothes. It's a million degrees outside."

Gardy changed into shorts and the unfortunate *Florida Is Hawt* t-shirt he'd purchased in the airport gift shop. When he pinched the bridge of his nose against the headache-inducing sun, Bell offered him her sunglasses.

After they grabbed croissant breakfast sandwiches, Bell led the way to the village park. Except for a mother and toddler using the swing set, the park was empty when Bell and Gardy grabbed a bench beside a tennis court. Gardy scanned the street, stopping on the parking garage. Too many places for a sniper to hide.

The injured, betrayed look in Gardy's eyes felt like a kick to Bell's stomach. He'd devoted his adult life to serving his country, always playing by the rules, and now he couldn't trust the BAU or his elected officials.

"You know I don't have a weapon," Gardy said. "TSA frowns on that sort of thing."

Gardy needed the FBI to submit an armed travel request allowing him to bring the Glock. No way he could have done so without alerting Weber.

"I have a backup weapon."

"What? Why?"

"Remember I bought another Glock after Weber suspended me?"

Gardy scratched his head.

"Yeah, I remember. If I'm going to break the rules, I might as well go for broke. Tell me why the senator wants Wolf dead."

"Wolf talked to the wrong people about Ewing, and the senator found out," Bell said, watching the mother give the swing a shove.

Gardy picked at a dandelion and tossed the flower into the grass.

"Why not order the hit on Wolf? Take him out and Ewing is free and clear."

"You know the answer, Gardy. A man like Logan Wolf isn't easily killed. Better to frame him, turn Wolf's own people against him."

"So Ewing hires someone to kill Renee and makes it look like Wolf did it."

Bell wrapped the rest of her breakfast and set it aside.

"And he makes the murder appear ritualistic, convincing Wolf a serial killer targeted his wife."

"But we don't have a single witness to corroborate the congresswoman's assertions. And there's no telling how many people this involves."

Bell leveled her eyes with Gardy's.

"We know one person who's involved. Don Weber."

Gardy deliberately set his breakfast down on the park bench.

"This again?"

"His sole focus is Logan Wolf. It's not an obsession. Weber didn't care about bringing Wolf to justice. He wants Wolf out of the way because Wolf has information on him."

"Care to elaborate?"

"I'm still connecting the dots, but I guarantee Weber is protecting Senator Ewing. You said so yourself a thousand times—the government promoted Weber beyond his competency. Could be Ewing agreed to push for Weber's promotion if the deputy director buried Wolf's case against him."

"So why do Ewing and Weber want us dead?"

Bell scrutinized the shrubs bordering the park. She felt eyes on her.

"Because Weber knows Wolf helped me at Blackwater Lake and in New York, and Weber is afraid we'll share information and blow him out of the water. That explains why Agent Flanagan followed us. I think I'll call Harold and have him query the 2013 database for any documents pertaining to Logan and Renee Wolf."

Gardy leaned back and locked his fingers behind his neck. The corners of his mouth tilted upward, suggesting Bell's conspiracy theories had hit a new level of ridiculousness. But his mind worked behind his eyes. Missing puzzle pieces fell into place.

"There's one way to prove Weber and Ewing tried to kill us," Gardy said, cocking his eyebrow.

"Go on."

Gardy chewed the last of the croissant and tossed the wrapper in the trash.

"Let's catch a sniper."

CHAPTER FOURTEEN

Larrabee shot Gardy a perfunctory look. No doubt the special agent's touristy clothes tampered her enthusiasm for Bell's partner. The detective's eyes glistened with intensity. Bell thought she could read Larrabee's doubts as if flipping a magazine open.

Detective Larrabee joined the Fair Haven Beach PD twelve years ago and found the department dominated by white males. They'd confined Larrabee to small cases, a quiet prejudice aimed at keeping her low on the totem pole. But she won the respect of her colleagues and rose through the ranks to detective on talent and steadfast persistence.

Larabee swiveled her gaze between the two agents.

"Tell me why you brought me here."

They sat at a long wooden table with years of scribbles etched into the surface. Bell preferred the neutral ground of the community college library. She didn't want Larrabee's colleagues overhearing what they had to say.

Florescent strip lighting hummed overhead. Two female students strolled among the stacks, and Bell waited until they moved on before she slid the FBI reports to

Larrabee detailing the congresswoman's assassination and the attempted murders of Gardy and Bell on the Chesapeake Bay. Larrabee set the two documents beside each other and moved her eyes between each, comparing.

"The assassination upset me," Larrabee said, turning the documents face-down. "San Giovanni was a beacon of hope for a lot of us. I buy your argument that the same shooter tried to kill you after you aided the congresswoman. But I fail to see what this has to do with my case."

Bell knew bringing Larrabee into the fold was a huge risk. If the detective dismissed the claims, she might contact Weber. But as Bell laid out her argument, the doubt vanished from Larrabee's face. The detective's eyes sharpened at the mention of Senator Ewing. Bell handed Larrabee the iPad.

"Agent Gardy discovered an encrypted document on the congresswoman's home computer. One of her sources claimed Ewing orchestrated Senator Klein's death, and I'm convinced Deputy Director Weber works for Ewing. I already confirmed Logan Wolf was the only BAU agent who pursued the Ewing case. "

Hearing Wolf's name rattled Larrabee. A female librarian pushed a cart of books past the table. When the woman turned the corner, Larrabee leaned forward.

"The FBI report implicates Wolf in his sister's death. Tell me the truth, Agent Bell. Is Wolf in my village?"

"Yes, but I assure you he didn't murder Christina Wolf. She was his only family."

"You must know Logan Wolf well if you can speak to his character. That concerns me."

"Nobody at this table trusts Logan Wolf," Gardy said,

breaking in. Bell looked at him in warning. "But I agree with Agent Bell. He didn't murder his sister. Another killer did."

Larrabee dropped her pen on the desk.

"Two serial killers. Any more good news you want to share with me?"

"Look, we aren't asking you to alter your investigation," Bell said. "Continue searching for Christina Wolf's murderer as you have with full support from the FBI."

"And by *FBI* you mean the two of you, not Deputy Director Weber."

"Yes."

"So what do you want from me?"

"Work with us. If I'm right, we'll catch Christina Wolf's killer and the man who tried to shoot Gardy and me."

"What makes you think the sniper is in Fair Haven Beach?"

"Because the attempt on our lives felt desperate. Weber and Ewing know we're gathering evidence to bring them down, and Wolf is at the center of the conspiracy."

Bell suggested a plan to lure the sniper out of hiding. Larrabee chewed on the idea for a long time before locking eyes with Bell.

"So you want me to turn you in to the FBI. Risky. If this plan blows up in your faces, you'll both go to jail."

As Bell continued, Gardy shifted uncomfortably. Bell hadn't shared her plan with him until now.

"Phone Don Weber and suggest your concerns about the way I'm handling this case, ensuring you mention Gardy is here. In the meantime, I'll plant an idea in his head."

"Explain."

"There's a man who follows my cases. A reporter named Gavin Hayward."

"I've never heard of him. Is he with *The Times* or *The Post*?"

"Neither. He writes for a gossip rag called *The Informer*."

Larrabee's mouth twisted.

"Yes, I'm aware of *The Informer*."

"Hayward begged me for the inside scoop for months. I'll tell him we're meeting with Logan Wolf and give him a location of our choice. As soon as Hayward releases the news, the BAU will find out. Weber and Ewing can't resist an opportunity to kill all three of us."

Larrabee drummed her fingers on the desk and looked up at the lights.

"What a world we live in where a snake like Ewing can elevate himself to the top of the government. But as much as I admired Congresswoman San Giovanni, this document is conjecture and hearsay. I'm going out on a limb for you."

"When this is over, you'll be the detective who captured a government assassin and Christina Wolf's murderer."

"I should bring my partner in on this. Vargus is on the fast track to detective, and he knows how to keep a secret."

"Sorry, I can't take the chance. Keep this plan between the three of us."

Larrabee released a held breath and closed her eyes.

"Okay, Agent Bell. I'm giving you forty-eight hours to prove you aren't insane."

The Redeemer

CHAPTER FIFTEEN

He hides inside a study cubicle in the library, one wide and bloodshot eye leering at them between the door and jamb.

Now and then a student passes the cubicle and interrupts his concentration. The males he ignores. His eyes linger on the girls. Young and beautiful, so much like the dozens of girls he's claimed as his own. It would be easy, so easy, to take one today. Follow her across campus and discover where she lives. Dormitory doors are cheaply constructed and flimsy, and the pathways between the dorms and quad are dark and poorly lit compared to large university campuses. This is his hunting ground.

There will be time for the girls after. When he's finished.

Scarlett Bell's legs cross under the table, and she tosses her hair back as he struggles to read the female agent's lips. Something about catching a serial killer. The thought amuses him. He's read about the men she captured, but she's never met one like him. He'll enjoy cutting her open and sealing her inside the container.

Keeping her forever.

But the ebony-skinned detective pulls his attention. She equals Scarlett Bell's beauty. He hadn't banked on the detective's presence, nor the male agent beside Scarlett. They pose new problems he must eliminate. First, the sensual detective. He'll deal with the man later.

Christina Wolf's killer, the ghost who haunts America's plains and its coasts, cities, farms, and forests, remains as patient as a stone on the bottom of a river. He waits until the three stand up from the table and agree to meet later. Except one of them won't be alive by then.

The door whispers open on well-oiled hinges. As the three targets descend the stairs, his shadow passes across the bookcases and leaves a chill in its wake. Merging with a group of students chatting with a professor, he follows the detective through the quad after she splits from the two agents. Curvy hips fill her skirt. Heels click the concrete walkway while she hustles toward the parking lot to escape the heat.

She clicks the key fob while he presses against his van, the baked aluminum searing his flesh. Good. She drove her own car, not a police cruiser. That means she's off the clock. The police won't expect her back at the office.

He whispers her plate number three times and commits it to memory in case he loses her in traffic. When she closes her car door, he lifts himself into the van and follows her onto the thoroughfare, always careful to keep a few vehicles between them.

The chase takes them through the center of the village and away from the ocean. The houses shrink as though they lack the water to sustain them, and the well-manicured lawns give way to bare patches where the grass wilts under

77

the unforgiving sun. Another stroke of luck. Fewer security systems stand in his way.

The woman pulls into a driveway, the blacktop crumbling with disrepair. She locks the car and carries her bag around the back of a small coral-painted two-story, pausing on the steps to glance back at the black van idling curbside. Did she see him in her mirrors?

Without giving the van a second glance, the detective unlocks the door and disappears inside.

Now he waits for dark.

***

Detective Larrabee didn't anticipate the anxiety she experienced when she phoned Don Weber at the FBI's Behavior Analysis Unit. She couldn't recall the last time she deceived another member of the law enforcement community, and Deputy Director Weber had the power to ruin her career if he suspected.

Weber came off as affable. Larrabee surmised he strove to make favorable initial impressions with the police departments his unit assisted, but she sensed a shark swimming beneath the surface. This was a man whose next move always strengthened his position.

He thanked Larrabee for expressing her concerns over Scarlett Bell's profile, and she felt him bristle over the phone when Agent Gardy's name came up. Larrabee only hoped Bell knew what she was doing.

She flipped the television on and kicked off her heels, then seeing nothing good was on, she shut down the TV and returned to the kitchen. Searching through the refrigerator, she settled on a yogurt and padded back to the living room with the snack. Thick drapes shut out the sun and concealed the junk pile marring her neighbor's fenced-in front yard. This had been a nice neighborhood when she inherited the little house from her mother, and now it attracted drug users and a criminal element. Last year, her arms full with grocery bags, she heard a distinct racial slur from across the street. When she turned, she found Mr. Randolph on his front porch rocking chair, beer in hand, stained wife-beater tank drooping off his shoulders. The son-of-a-bitch lifted his middle finger when she stared too long. If he was willing to harass a cop, how would he treat another minority family?

A scratching noise against the siding caught her attention. Yanking the curtains back, she craned her head and searched the driveway. Satisfied nobody was messing with her car, she shut the curtains and checked the back door lock.

Sighing, she set the empty yogurt cup down and climbed the stairs. The bedroom was darker than the living room. She used blackout curtains so she could sleep on overnight shifts. A box fan in the corner buzzed with white noise, a sound she'd grown so accustomed to she never turned the fan off. She kept her bedroom military-neat, no laundry to trip over, the bedspread smooth as calm waters while she fished sweatpants out of the dresser. A gilded photograph of her mother and father, both gone for five years now, stood beside a jewelry box on the dresser. She touched the photo and silently asked them if she was doing the right thing, lying to one of the FBI's most powerful agents.

Eyeing the clock, Larrabee noted she had five hours until she met with Agents Bell and Gardy at her hotel. She set her alarm to go off in three hours and curled beneath the covers, the extra pillow draped over her ear to block out the neighborhood clamor.

Larrabee didn't sleep long.

When she sprang awake, she knew something was wrong. A sound. Someone outside…inside?…the house. Her body went rigid as though she'd fallen back on a sheet of ice.

Larrabee willed her legs to move. She drew down the blanket, the chill of the climate-controlled air coaxing her flesh to rise in goosebumps.

She reached out for her gun and remembered it was downstairs. With her phone.

Shit.

What was it she'd heard? Maybe nothing. Just the slam of a car door or one of her neighbors cursing.

She lay her head back on the pillow and strained to listen as the box fan drowned out the outside world. That's when she knew she wasn't alone in the house.

Larrabee crept down from the bed and slid along the wall, searching for something, anything on her desk that would serve as a weapon. The metal jewelry box had sharp edges. It wasn't enough to kill a man, but if she brought it down at the right angle, the box would excavate a chunk of flesh and make the intruder think twice about fighting.

Lifting the box, she moved on cat's paws to the door. She slid the door open a crack to see if anyone was on the landing.

Empty.

She exhaled a moment before a thumping noise came from behind. Inside the closet.

Larrabee spun around.

And saw the wide, psychotic eye glaring at her through the cracked open door.

She screamed and turned to run when he lunged. His hand grabbed her hair and yanked, snapping her neck back. Her feet flew out from under her, legs splayed as he climbed atop her stomach. She swung the jewelry box and knocked his head sideways. Blood trickled down his forehead as she brought the box back for another swing.

A powerful hand shot down and gripped her neck. Squeezed. Eyes wide and desperate, she slammed the jewelry box against his head and scraped flesh and hair away from his scalp.

Eyes rolling back, the maniac toppled over and collapsed on the floor. Larrabee screamed for help as she squirmed to get out from under him. She still lay beneath his dead weight.

Coughing, she slipped one leg free and slammed her foot into his ribs. He struggled back to his knees as she kicked out again and stung his chin, whipping his head back.

Crawling on all fours, Larrabee struggled toward the closed bedroom door. She reached the threshold, but he grabbed her ankle and dragged her back into the bedroom.

She beat her fists against his face and drove the point of her elbow against his neck. But he didn't flinch.

The backhand slap stunned her. She stumbled backward, the room spinning, floor rising to meet her. Larrabee's head struck the wall. Stars flashed in her eyes as she swung blindly.

Then the maniac wrapped his hands around her throat and lifted. Suspended off the floor, eye-to-eye with the maniac, her legs kicked at him as he squeezed the life out of her.

With one hand, he propped her against the wall like a rag doll. The other hand reached behind him and removed the knife, razor sharp and bloodstained.

She knew who he was now. Christina Wolf's serial killer. Peering into his eyes opened a window to the bodies he'd left behind. He was more than a murderer. He was a dark legend. A whisper told at midnight to frighten children. Nothing could stop him.

He came here to kill Larrabee. After he snuffed out the last remaining light in her body, he'd butcher Scarlett Bell. And Neil Gardy.

And any mortal fool enough to stand against him.

CHAPTER SIXTEEN

The conversation with Gavin Hayward of *The Informer* left Bell queasy as if a thick sheen of brown grease slicked her skin.

But the bait was set. Though she discerned Hayward's doubt—he didn't understand why she'd contact him with classified information—the rat snatched the cheese. Now she only had to wait until the story went live on the tabloid's website.

Outside the hotel room window, the brutal heat waned, and daylight took on orange and red tints. The sun dropped below a line of palms through the west window.

"You sure about this?" Gardy asked, checking his gun.

She wasn't. How could she be certain about a plan she'd cobbled together in a few hours?

A text from Larrabee sat in Bell's phone. As agreed upon, the detective had called Weber and planted the seed that something was wrong in Fair Haven Beach. The instant he found out about *The Informer* article, he'd contact the sniper and order the executions. But Larrabee hadn't answered any of Bell's texts since.

Bell fed Hayward a vague description of the meeting site so the public wouldn't figure it out. She didn't want a hundred vigilantes to wreck her plan. But Weber would recognize the location a mile from the beach house where the serial killer murdered Christina Wolf.

The location seemed perfect: unless the sniper broke into a populated home along the beach, the only hiding spot with an unobstructed shot was the cluster of palms and scrub on the north end of the beach. That's where Bell would wait.

"I'm calling the police," Bell finally said, taking one last peek through the curtains. She spotted a shadow in the parking garage. It might have been anybody, a shopper searching for his car after closing time. But the dark presence set her on edge as she searched for the black van she'd seen yesterday.

"Larrabee is on her day off," Gardy said, holstering the gun. "Could be she wanted to unwind this evening. Or maybe she got cold feet after calling Weber."

"It doesn't feel right. I'm worried about her."

Bell sneaked another look between the curtains. No sign of the man in the parking garage.

The officer who answered the phone sounded at his wit's end as a man, probably someone the police arrested, yelled about his rights in the background. He huffed as Bell explained her concerns. Despite his reservations, the officer agreed to send a cruiser past Larrabee's house.

After thanking the officer, Bell refreshed the main page of *The Informer* on her phone. The short article headlined the page in bold letters. *FBI's Scarlett Bell Meeting Serial Killer Logan Wolf.* She clicked the article and

skimmed the text, catching two typos in the rushed article.
Hayward had come through.

"Hayward published the article," Bell said, sliding the
phone into her back pocket. "Let's give Weber ten minutes
to call his mercenary."

"It won't take him that long."

Gardy's phone rang as they prepared to leave. He
mouthed, "It's Harold," while the analyst fed him the
information he'd dug up on Weber and Logan Wolf.

"Send me the document, Harold," Gardy said. "And I
want you to send a copy to an attorney I know...right...
here's his contact information."

Gardy read Harold the information and gave a
thumbs-up to Bell.

"We've got Weber," Gardy said when the call ended.
"He ordered surveillance on Logan and Renee Wolf in
2013. The bastard knew the wife's daily routine down to
the minute."

"Good move sending copies."

"Not that anything bad will happen to Harold."

"Or us?"

Purple gloaming made the village seem alien and
otherworldly as Bell and Gardy descended the steps and
crossed the vacated thoroughfare. With the shops closed,
the village seemed like a ghost town. She half-expected
tumbleweed roll across the road.

Entering the parking garage prickled her skin again.
Gardy glared at her when she pulled to a stop on the
second level.

"What's wrong?"

She swung her eyes through the garage, past the
concrete beams to the darkness gathering along the far wall.

"Nothing. Let's go."

Gardy remained silent during the ride across the village. This was how he acted when a case made him nervous. She kept checking the mirrors, expecting to see a trailing vehicle, but the roads remained empty except for a few cars entering parking lots for big box stores and chain restaurants. Bell caught herself gripping the steering wheel and eased off, forcing herself to regulate her breathing. The plan seemed foolhardy as they approached the coast. She feared for Gardy, the senior agent who'd looked after Bell through her first years with the BAU. An unwanted memory flashed in her mind—Gardy bent over the steering wheel, head dripping blood after they crashed in Coral Lake, New York. She didn't know what she'd do without him in her life.

He caught her staring.

"We always find a way," Gardy said, sensing her doubt. "Stay focused on what we need to do. It's a solid plan."

It isn't, she thought. Too many loose ends, too much potential for the case to blow up in their faces. And she couldn't shake the feeling that someone had followed her since she arrived in Fair Haven Beach.

The beach house came into view when she rounded a dogleg curve that deposited them onto the coast road. The steepled roof looked like a shark fin. Yellow crime scene tape glowed in the fading light.

Bell parked along the road, and they walked down to the palm grove, unconcerned about anyone seeing the rental car. She wanted to announce her presence, make sure the sniper knew where to find them.

Guns in hand, they sifted through the trees. Nobody

was here. Good. They had time to scope out the area before the sniper arrived.

Dusk turned to dark, and the dark turned black and oily. A brisk wind off the ocean tickled the fronds and hurled breakers against the sand. But still no sign of the shooter.

"Where do you think you're going?" Bell asked when Gardy left their hiding spot and headed toward the beach.

"We're supposed to be meeting Logan Wolf. Somebody needs to play the part, and I'm a more convincing male."

She wanted to say something snarky. Break the tension threatening to tear them in half. She couldn't. The words died on Bell's lips when he abandoned her.

Then she barely saw him anymore as he merged with the night. He holstered his gun and concealed it beneath his t-shirt as he paced the beach. Gardy stopped near the shoreline and waited. Solemn as a statue.

She never heard the footsteps approach from behind.

CHAPTER SEVENTEEN

The callused hand covered Bell's mouth and yanked her backward. She swung her elbow back at his head, but her assailant ducked the blow and placed a knife against her throat.

"Shh," her abductor said, whispering in her ear.

His forearm clamped against her chest and held her in place. She sank her teeth into his flesh. No effect. The man didn't flinch.

Powerful arms spun her around, and she stared into the black, depthless eyes of Logan Wolf. He placed his forefinger against his lips and pointed past the trees. At first, she didn't see anything. Then stone crackled underfoot as someone approached along the gravel shoulder off the coast road.

The wicked edge of his knife poised beneath her chin. But he made no move to sweep the blade through her flesh. Instead, he tilted his head, an indication he wanted her to circle around the grove.

A shadow drifted among the trees. Deadly and silent. She spotted the rifle a moment before the man ducked out of sight.

Her heart hammered. Gardy stood inside the shooter's scope. A sitting duck.

"He won't shoot yet," Wolf said, his face close to hers. "He wants all three of us."

Bell nodded. How the hell did Wolf know their plan? He must have followed Bell and Gardy. That would explain the sensation of being watched, but Bell sensed something darker in the night. Pure evil.

Wolf sheathed the knife and pushed her shoulder. "Go."

Bell moved on all fours through the grove. The wind and waves masked her progress, but she couldn't see the sniper anymore. Assuming the assassin set up his shot at the edge of the grove, Bell worked toward the beach. The sea breeze threw sand in her eyes, blurring her vision. Then she spied the barrel poking out from the trees. God, she'd almost crawled into the shooter.

She scurried back, afraid she'd spooked him, when another shadow closed in on the shooter from behind. Wolf.

On the beach, Gardy stood with his hands in his pockets. He kept them there so one hand stayed close to the Glock, but that wouldn't save him if the sniper pulled the trigger.

Wolf was close. Almost on top of the shooter.

The sniper sensed Wolf and spun around, but with his high-powered rifle centered on the beach, he couldn't defend himself. Wolf shoved the sniper to the ground and stuck the point of his blade into the soft flesh below the man's chin. Bell rushed out of hiding with the Glock aimed at the shooter.

"Don't kill him, Wolf."

"Why shouldn't I? He would have cut us down and never lost a minute of sleep."

"Do as I say."

Bell swung the gun at Wolf, and the serial killer shot her a wry smile before he pulled the knife back. Hearing the commotion, Gardy broke his cover and ran toward the grove. Bell turned her flashlight on the sniper.

"You the one who shot at us in Virginia?" she asked, pulling the rifle out of the man's reach. When he didn't answer, she stepped down on his hand, eliciting an angry moan as she pressed the Glock to his head. "Tell me who hired you."

Taking the flashlight from Bell, Gardy swept the beam over the shooter, hissing when he realized how close he came to being shot. He drew the Glock from his holster when he saw Wolf.

"How did Wolf find out about the meeting?"

"Apparently he reads the same websites as Weber," Bell said, grinding her foot down.

The shooter winced, but he refused to speak. Reaching down, Gardy ripped off the black hat and revealed the man's shaved head. Stubble dotted his face, his skin wrinkled and parched from too many years under the sun. Bell placed him in his forties.

"I'll make this easy for you," said Bell, kneeling so she was face-to-face with the shooter. "We're already aware Senator Ewing contracted you to murder us, and Don Weber at the FBI made the call. Give them up, and we'll let you live."

"I don't know what you're talking about."

The man's voice was hoarse and gravely. His smug

grin stretched the width of his face.

"The last man who tried to shoot me ended up with a bullet in his forehead. Right here." Bell jammed her finger above the man's eyebrows. "Why protect Ewing and Weber? They'll toss you away after they finish with you. Don't think they won't sell you out to save themselves."

The man spat. The glob landed on her sneaker.

"Nice," she said, wiping her sneaker off in the sand.

"You aren't gonna do shit," he said, grinning. "You're federal agents. What will the government say if you shoot an unarmed man?"

"Check him," Bell said.

Gardy searched the man's pockets and shook his head. Except for the rifle, the man came unarmed.

"See? What did I tell you? Haul me into jail for aiming a rifle at the surf."

"You aimed at my partner."

"Prove it."

Wolf lurked in the shadows, his gaze fixed on the shooter. He lifted his eyes to Bell, and an unspoken agreement passed between them.

"You'll give us a full confession," Bell said, smiling. "I'm going to enjoy this."

"Stupid bitch. Place me under arrest or let me walk."

"Your benefactors marched you into a meat grinder. Allow me to introduce you to a man Don Weber ordered you to shoot tonight. His name is Logan Wolf. Does that name mean anything to you?"

Gardy glanced at Bell and opened his mouth. She shook her head. The sniper kept grinning, but uncertainty leaked into his eyes.

"Maybe you've heard of him. He's the FBI agent who

went rogue in 2013 and became the nation's most wanted serial killer. Does that ring a bell?"

The sniper's eyes moved between Bell and Wolf.

"I don't believe you."

"He slaughtered dozens of men we know of. Who knows how many more? Wolf slit their throats and spilled their blood, then he placed sacks over their heads. Rumor has it he hides their faces so the spirits of the deceased can't look at him anymore."

When the man's stoic expression failed, Wolf snaked a hand into his pocket and removed the sack.

"This is insane, Bell," Gardy said, rounding on her. "We can't stand by while Wolf murders this guy, no matter how reprehensible he is."

"Then we won't watch," she said, lowering the gun as Wolf slid the knife against the sniper's throat. "Come on, Gardy."

Wolf's eyes smiled back at Bell as she left him alone with the gunman. The man's protests turned to screams as Bell and Gardy walked away.

CHAPTER EIGHTEEN

Whirling lights painted blues and angry reds against Detective Larrabee's house. A throng of neighbors came outside to watch, some holding beers and claiming the bitch got what she had coming, others wide-eyed and covering their mouths with their hands as the crime techs ascended the front steps, little baggies covering their shoes.

Officer Vargus, the policeman who'd accompanied Larrabee to the beach house and found Bell inside, stood in the doorway. His face looked pale and drawn, his eyes unfocused as he checked the credentials of everyone entering the house. The first on the scene, he'd discovered Larrabee in the upstairs bedroom, the walls and carpet soaked with blood. The memory of Larrabee's bloody outline against the wall was one he couldn't exorcise. As though the killer hoisted the detective to the ceiling before he tore her to pieces.

Chief Sahd, gray-haired and harried after the emergency called him away from dinner night with his wife, nodded at the two crime techs passing him.

"She upstairs?" When Vargus only glared at Sahd, the

chief touched his shoulder. "Vargus, what happened here?"

"Don't go up there, Chief. You don't want to see what he...Jesus, it doesn't even look like her."

Sahd nodded grimly and pushed past, but the chief would probably clamor down the stairs a minute later. Vargus would give Sahd points if the man didn't vomit in the bushes.

The hulking officer felt as if he'd shrunk several inches since arriving at Larrabee's. He studied the onlookers, most of them looky-loos and rubberneckers who wanted to glimpse a dead cop. They'd have to wait a long time. The CSI team had a helluva mess to sift through.

Vargus bit his tongue over the thought. That *mess* upstairs was his partner, a woman he admired. To Vargus, Larrabee seemed bulletproof, invincible. The murderer who killed her was no ordinary man. He was a demon wearing human skin.

Another squad car arrived as Vargus scanned the crowd. Fair Haven Beach didn't attract serial killers. He recalled a handful of murders during his ten years on the force. But he knew enough to suspect the killer stood among the crowd. Blending in. Watching. He studied the faces, passing over animated expressions of horror and elation and honing in on the rapt and silent. These were the most likely killers among the mob. The faces of death.

A hand grabbed his shoulder, and Vargus swiveled around to Chief Sahd staring at him. Sahd looked as if he'd aged twenty years since viewing the murder scene.

"You have any idea who did this to her, Officer?"

Vargus couldn't focus. His attention kept drifting back to the crowd.

"Vargus, who did this?"

Shaking his head, Vargus guarded the door as the medical examiner's car pulled to the curb.

"Larrabee got in over her head with that FBI agent."

"Agent Bell?" Sahd narrowed his eyes. "Are you saying there's more going on than this serial killer case?"

"Just a feeling. Detective Larrabee held nothing back, but she hid her activities after that agent arrived."

"The killer targeted one of ours, Officer, and I want him caught before sunrise. I'll handle the crime scene. You find this Agent Bell. I want to know what hell she dragged Detective Larrabee into."

CHAPTER NINETEEN

Gardy cringed every time the sniper squealed. Bell did her best to block out the horror, to compartmentalize the unthinkable. She couldn't. It sounded like Wolf was carving a live pig inside the grove.

She looked up when the vegetation parted. Two shadowed men shuffled toward the road. Wolf clutched the unknown man by his jacket, keeping the shooter on his feet.

"His name is Grant Schlosser, and he's prepared to make a full confession, including the fire he started at your apartment and the bomb he placed under your SUV."

Wolf tossed Schlosser forward, and he fell against Bell's rental, his hands leaving bloody palm prints on the trunk. He lacked part of one ear, and a long, gory trench cut from Schlosser's cheek toward his eye.

"We can't take his confession like this," Gardy said. "This is torture."

"As long as he implicates Ewing and Weber," Bell said. "I'll sleep like a baby, regardless."

Gardy wore an incredulous look on his face. He didn't want any part of Wolf's confession methods.

"This isn't the man who killed my sister," Wolf said, jabbing the point of the knife against Schlosser's jugular. "But I bet he knows who did."

Schlosser's Adam's apple bounced as he swallowed hard.

"I know other men are involved, but I don't know names."

"You lie."

"I swear."

"They paid you well, I trust," Bell said, lifting the shooter's chin to examine his wounds. "They better have, because your pain is just beginning if I find out you're lying."

Gardy opened the back door. Bell shoved Schlosser inside. Fixing the gun on Schlosser, Gardy slid into the backseat beside him.

Bell gazed at Wolf in the moonlight. Determination and hate lit a fire in the serial killer's eyes, yet his shoulders slumped with the exhaustion of a man who'd shouldered horror for too many years.

"You'd do well to disappear, Wolf. This time forever. I'll clear your name in Renee's murder, and Ewing and Weber will pay for what they did to us, but I can't protect you."

"This night doesn't end until I find Christina's killer."

"Sorry, Wolf. You're not coming with us. You found your way here, so I assume you have transportation nearby. Get in your car and drive. Don't stop until you find a coast you don't recognize."

"Such a shame our time together must end. We could have made an incredible team, the two of us. Imagine what we could accomplish if we fought on the same side."

"I'll never be like you."

"You already are."

Bell shifted her feet. She sensed Gardy's eyes on her from inside the car.

"Remember what I told you. This is your only chance if you want to remain a free man. I need to go."

Bell turned away. Wolf clutched her shoulder and spun her around. She stared into his eyes, two lost souls peering back at her. Her breath quickened, fingers sliding toward the Glock.

When he pressed his lips to hers, she fell back against the door, head swimming with a million reasons to push him away.

She didn't.

His kiss rippled warmth through her body, sent pins-and-needles down her legs. When he pulled away, she'd lost track of time. He strode into the dark, a low chuckle riding the wind as he disappeared.

"Until we meet again, Agent Bell."

Bell touched the door handle and waited. The silhouettes of Gardy and Schlosser in the backseat barely registered in her mind. Finally, she tugged the door open and slid behind the wheel. As she fired the engine, Gardy's eyes found hers in the mirror. She looked away before the hurt grew unbearable.

Bell pulled onto the road and turned the car around. The sooner she brought Schlosser to the police station, the better. She wanted this nightmare to end. After the courts convicted Weber and Ewing, she'd call it a day. Walk away from law enforcement, corruption, and murderers forever. She was young enough to enter another field. Maybe follow her parents to Arizona and forget the last two years happened.

The village lights glittered in the distance when the van rammed them from the side. Tires screeched. Then the car spun across the median and flipped into the ditch.

Her vision spun. The scent of burned rubber met her nose as she struggled to work the feeling back into her legs.

The spiderweb of fractured windshield caved in toward her face.

"Gardy?"

No answer. She tried to turn her head, but agony stopped her dead.

A door opened and shut. Footsteps.

Bell searched for her gun and found it on her hip, but her body lay wrenched around the steering wheel, preventing her from retrieving the weapon.

"Gardy, wake up!"

The door flew open. Hands groped inside and tugged at her arm. The seat belt, the only reason she was still alive, held her fast. The madman severed the straps with his knife and hauled her from the vehicle. She collapsed against the blacktop, body screaming as he reached for her again.

He hoisted Bell by the neck and threw her into the ditch. Rocks tore at her back. She scrambled to her hands and knees, but he was too fast. Relentless.

His arm clubbed the back of her head and turned the world upside down. A boot caught her under the chin and snapped her neck back with a spray of blood.

As she rolled onto her back, he pocketed the knife and produced a camera with a glowing screen. The brightness seared her eyes, but when she tried to look away, the madman snatched her chin and forced her to look.

And Bell saw Larrabee's butchered body, the detective's blank eyes staring accusingly.

She swung her leg and struck his ankle, tripping him up. His arms pinwheeled before he slammed shoulder-first against the blacktop.

The maneuver bought her enough time to retrieve the Glock before he sprang to his feet. She squeezed the trigger. The bullet punctured the madman's shoulder and knocked him against the van. She recognized the vehicle from the parking garage. Several large bulks stood behind tinted windows. A shiver rolled through Bell as she imagined what lay inside the barrels.

One hand clutching his shoulder, blood spilling between his fingers, the killer battled back to his feet. She squeezed off a second shot. It sailed wide and took out the van's side mirror. He stalked across the dividing line while Bell dragged herself to the shoulder. He kicked the gun from her hand when she tried to center the weapon, and it skidded through the gravel and came to rest in a patch of weed and tall grass growing in a bordering meadow.

Bell scurried after the lost weapon. He grabbed her ankle and dragged her into the road.

The blade caught the starlight as he leered down at her.

"Come home, little one. Time to sleep."

The knife flashed at her face when another gun blast thundered over her head. The killer flew backward and landed on his elbows. A fresh wound bubbled blood from his thigh. Bell twisted her head. Gardy slumped over the ruined car, the undercarriage steadying his grip on the Glock. The next shot sailed past the killer and blew a hole through the van. Losing his balance, Gardy tumbled to the pavement.

The scuff of boot against blacktop was the only warning Bell received as the killer loomed over her. Powerful hands gripped her hair and yanked. She slid across the road, the cruel surface tearing her knees while she fought to spin away.

With one hand he threw the van door open, the other buried in her hair and ripping locks from her scalp. The van trembled as he stepped inside. An overwhelming death scent rolled out of the vehicle. Now inside the van, he dug both hands into her hair and tugged. Her body lifted off the pavement as her neck arced backward.

She landed inside the death van. Eyes glassed over, she stared at the doubled visions of barrels stacked along the walls. This was the end. He was too powerful.

The growl of another motor pulled the killer's eyes to the road. An SUV skidded to a halt and fishtailed toward the van. Bumpers slammed, and the killer toppled onto the macadam as Bell cleared her head. She prayed the police had arrived, but she knew better. Wolf came back for her.

Knives cut through the air. Bell slumped against a barrel as something shifted inside. While she blocked out the image of what lay inside the barrels, Gardy yelled from across the road. He'd pulled himself onto the overturned car again and aimed the Glock at the two serial killers.

"Move!" Gardy yelled, motioning Bell to get out of the line of fire.

"No, Gardy. You'll shoot Wolf!"

Wolf yelled out and stumbled. A red line formed and soaked his shirt. The maniac swept the knife at Wolf when Gardy's gunshot caught the killer's arm. He spun toward Gardy, an unstoppable force. Before Gardy could fire again, the killer clutched his neck and squeezed. Gardy's eyes bulged, tongue lolled out as the killer lifted him off the ground and the gun tumbled from his hand. The agent beat his fists against the maniac's face. The killer grinned, his teeth stained red.

Though every bone in her body begged her to stop, Bell pushed herself out of the van and across the road. Wolf circled from behind. Together, they closed in on the killer. Gardy's neck appeared on the brink of snapping when Bell leaped atop the killer's back and raked her nails across his eyes. He threw her off, yet she'd freed Gardy, who lay crumpled in the road. Was he breathing?

Bell sprang up and slammed her fist against the killer's face. The maniac's eyes crossed a moment before Wolf drove the knife into his back. As the killer slumped over, Bell leaped and wrapped her thighs around his neck. He landed on his knees and brought his head up. For a split-second they locked eyes. Then Bell twisted her hips and snapped his neck.

The killer twitched once and lay still.

Bell crawled away. She kept imagining the killer's hands around her neck as she touched her throat and glanced over at Gardy. Her partner's chest swelled and receded. Thank God.

She struggled over to Gardy and supported his head in her lap.

"He's dead, Gardy. Everything will be all right. You can open your eyes now."

Gardy remained unresponsive as Bell brushed the hair from his eyes and felt his neck for a pulse.

"He needs help, Wolf. Can you drive?"

When she turned her head, Wolf had disappeared.

Her eyes swept across the road and stopped on Christina's killer. Someone had slit his throat and slid a black sack over his head.

Wolf's stolen SUV butted up against the killer's van, the front ends mangled. All around her, night closed in on the lonely roadway. Crickets sang to the stars, and somewhere a cicada buzzed.

"Wolf?"

But he was gone. She wondered if she'd ever see him again.

CHAPTER TWENTY

Bell clutched her aching head and peeked between the Venetian blinds into the interrogation room.

Throwing their weight around, the Fair Haven Beach police had seized control of the Grant Schlosser case. They wouldn't have control for long. The FBI would rip the case away once they determined Schlosser's violent crimes crossed state lines. And when they discovered he'd murdered Congresswoman San Giovanni, the feds would nab Schlosser and never let go.

Behind the glass, Chief Sahd and Officer Vargus interviewed Schlosser. Bell smirked at the good cop, bad cop routine when Sahd slammed his fists down on the desk and knocked over a chair. Bell knew the sniper saw her through the glass. He wouldn't look her in the eye.

She checked her texts and found nothing new. Gardy had been at the hospital for three hours. The prognosis— four busted ribs, a concussion, and a sprained neck. He was lucky to be alive. They all were.

Another hour passed. Sometimes Sahd questioned Schlosser, other times Vargus drew the short straw.

Together, they filled multiple pages of notebook paper with Schlosser's statements. Bell knew the sniper would tell the truth. Wolf was still out there, and he'd find Schlosser if the shooter didn't confess.

A pall hung over the office. Detective Larrabee weighed on the officers' minds, but each cop tilted his cap when he met Bell's eyes. Executing a cop killer won their respect.

The atmosphere grew darker inside the interrogation room. Sahd and Vargus met eyes and glanced back at Bell. After a moment, Sahd strode into the operations area and snatched Bell by the elbow, ushering her into his office. He locked the door. The silence rang in Bell's ears.

"You realize who Schlosser just implicated," Sahd said, standing behind his desk and leaning forward on his arms.

"I do."

"Jesus H…Senator Ewing and the Deputy Director of CIRG. The assassination of a U.S. congresswoman? How did this war converge on my village?"

Vargus, the first police officer to arrive at the coast road, had identified the serial killer. Greg Maxey, a traveling salesman working out of California. The first unlucky CSI tech to pry open a barrel lost her dinner on the blacktop. Their work had just begun. They'd spend a long time identifying the bodies and matching them to missing person cold cases.

"Do yourself a favor, Chief. Put Schlosser in holding and hand the case over to the feds. You know they'll take charge when they arrive."

Sahd scratched his forehead.

"I don't need this shit."

While two officers led Schlosser to the cells at the back of the office, Bell rubbed her eyes and wondered if Gardy was awake. Yet she couldn't stop thinking about Wolf. Though she couldn't justify Wolf stalking and murdering serial killers, she felt empathy. Ewing and Weber took everything from him. His wife, his freedom, his sanity. And now his last remaining family member. Had Bell been in the same position, she might have sought a similar vengeance on serial killers.

Bell collected her bag, expecting a wrap-up meeting with Sahd before she left for the hospital. The doors flew open. Bell's mouth went dry as Deputy Director Weber and Agent Flanagan strutted into the office.

"I want this woman arrested," Weber said, pointing at Bell.

The police officer Weber charged with arresting Bell was a thin, short man with a handlebar mustache. He glanced uncertainly at Sahd, who'd wandered out of his office to see what the commotion was.

"Did you hear me? Arrest this woman."

"On what grounds?" Sahd asked, moving to block Weber.

"Conspiring with a known fugitive and serial killer."

Sahd removed the cuffs from his hip as Weber grinned. The smile disappeared when Vargus grabbed Weber's arms and Sahd slapped the cuffs on the deputy director.

"Are you insane?"

"Don Weber, you're under arrest for conspiracy to murder a United States congresswoman," Vargus said. "You have the right to remain silent. Anything you say can and will be used against you in a court of law…"

Weber yanked at the cuffs as Vargus read his Miranda rights. As Flanagan edged away, Bell rounded the desk and ensured Weber's little helper didn't run.

"Chief Sahd," Bell said, rounding on Weber. "I'd like two minutes with the deputy director."

Sahd chewed on the idea before he agreed.

The chief led Weber into the interrogation room. Bell ensured no one looked in on them.

"You're in over your head," Weber said, leering at Bell. "These charges won't stick."

"Sit down," Bell said, pushing on Weber's shoulder.

The Deputy Director of CIRG stared darts into Bell as she drew up a chair and faced him.

"We uncovered BAU documents from 2013. They list Renee Wolf's nightly routine, cross-referenced with Logan Wolf's work schedule. This evidence is in the hands of an attorney firm which specializes in law enforcement corruption. When I'm done here, I'll make sure Congresswoman San Giovanni's task force members have their own copies. Should anything happen to Gardy or me, the firm will release the information to the US Attorney, the FBI, and the national media."

Weber raised his chin in defiance, but he swallowed when they locked eyes.

"You were always a disgrace to the BAU, Agent Bell."

"Unfortunately, you won't be in a position to accept my letter of resignation. Say hello to Senator Ewing for Lana when you get to prison."

The first glint of sunshine warmed the eastern sky when Bell arrived at the hospital.

His ribs bandaged, Gardy slept fitfully on the hospital

bed. Bell pulled a chair beside the bed and watched him. The senior agent wore a boyish expression as his eyes swiveled beneath closed lids. Dreaming of a better time and place.

Two orderlies chuckled in the hallway. Bell closed the door and settled into the chair. Checking her phone, she noticed a message from Harold from an hour ago. He wanted to know how Gardy was doing. Bell exhaled. Harold was safe. She returned a quick text and urged Harold to get out of Virginia for a few weeks. Take that vacation he'd put off all year.

Bell didn't realize she'd fallen asleep until the nurse brushed against her while checking on Gardy. As Bell straightened Gardy's blanket, her partner assessed her through thin slits for eyes.

"How are you feeling?" she asked, knowing it was a meaningless question. She could imagine the amount of pain he experienced.

"Doctor says the ribs will heal on their own, but it will take months before I'm myself. How about you?"

Bell shrugged. Her body ached as though she'd crashed a car and flipped into a ditch.

"I'll recover, but the rental company will be pissed."

Gardy gave his Muttley the cartoon dog snicker and clutched his ribs.

When they were alone again, Bell filled Gardy in on the night's proceedings. The Fair Haven Beach police arrested Weber and turned him over to the FBI. The rumor of Senator Ewing's impending arrest had leaked to the press.

"What about Wolf?" Gardy groaned.

"He's gone. For good this time, I think."

"Don't count on it."

"The crazy part is the momentum is on his side. The police cleared his name regarding Christina's death, and it's inevitable the FBI will do the same with his wife's murder. In the eyes of the law, he'll be an innocent man."

Gardy looked toward the window. The deep blue sky spoke of optimism and new beginnings.

"Sure, if you don't count the serial killers Wolf murdered."

Bell leaned closer and threw a glance over her shoulder. The door stood closed.

"There's a serious issue with those murders."

"Educate me."

"Wolf never left DNA. The FBI has surveillance footage of Wolf in the area for two murders, but they can't convict him on a couple random sightings. And his modus operandi?" Bell raised an eyebrow. "Turns out a certain serial killer used the same method to kill Wolf's wife and sister."

"And now that serial killer is dead, and the FBI thinks he's responsible for Wolf's murders. Very convenient for your friend."

Bell looked down. Her hands rested on the bed a few inches from his. A silence borne of lost opportunities and regrets passed between them. Sitting this close, Bell couldn't deny her feelings for Gardy. She wished once, just once, he'd shown the same interest in her. In recent months Gardy seemed on the verge of bonding with Bell. Gardy never followed through, and that told Bell he'd never take the next step.

"You're leaving the FBI," he said, dropping his eyes.

It wasn't a question. Bell had reached the end of the

road, and Gardy read the lack of direction and purpose in her eyes. She was lost.

"Yes."

He bit his lip and picked at an invisible piece of lint on the blanket. After a moment, he nodded.

"So this is the end. For us, I mean."

A tear tracked down her face. She'd entered the FBI to avenge her childhood best friend, a girl who died young after a serial killer stole her from the world. When the killer resurfaced, Bell ensured he'd never hurt anyone again. Through her brief career with the BAU, she always believed better days awaited her.

With Weber in jail and Ewing's arrest imminent, Bell accepted better days would never arrive while she worked for the FBI.

But she couldn't abandon Gardy now. He looked broken inside and out.

"You aren't getting rid of me that easily. I'll have plenty of free time. Who better to check on you while you rehabilitate your injuries?"

"No, you should go on with your life, Bell. Don't wait around for me. I'll only slow you down."

She stared down at her hands, wishing he'd asked her to stay. For him, she would have. Then she set her hands against the bed and stood.

"If you're certain."

"I'm certain I want you to be happy."

She turned and opened the door. Once she stepped outside of this room, there would be no turning back. They'd see each other at the criminal proceedings and the case debriefing, but the gap between them would be too large to bridge.

When she looked over her shoulder, Gardy's chin dropped to his chest.

"What if happiness means having you in my life?" Gardy asked.

Bell smiled. Maybe she'd stick around a little longer.

***

Thank you for being a loyal reader!

If you love dark psychological thrillers, read my new serial killer series, Darkwater Cove.

Darkwater Cove: Available on Amazon

Let the Party Begin!

I'm a pretty nice guy once you look past the grisly images in my head. Most of all, I love connecting with kickass readers like you.

Join the party and be part of my exclusive VIP Readers Group at:

WWW.DANPADAVONA.COM

The Redeemer

Show Your Support for Indie Thriller Authors

Did you enjoy this book? If so, please let other thriller fans know by leaving a short review. Positive reviews help spread the word about independent authors and their novels. Thank you.

The Redeemer

Why Novellas?

The world of entertainment has changed. While I enjoy movies, I watch Netflix series and comparable programming more frequently. Movies are too short to match the story and character arcs of a well-written series, and that's why I favor a long series of novellas over a few novels.

I prefer a long series which I can lose myself in, but broken up into smaller, manageable episodes that don't take up my entire evening.

In short, I'm writing the types of stories I enjoy and composing them into forms I find preferable.

I sincerely hope you enjoy the Scarlett Bell series as much as I love writing it.

How many episodes can you expect? Provided the series is well-received by readers, I don't foresee a definite end and would prefer to expand on the characters and plot lines for the foreseeable future. I still have plenty of devious ideas for upcoming stories.

Stay tuned!

The Redeemer

About the Author

Dan Padavona is the author of the The Scarlett Bell thriller series, Severity, The Dark Vanishings series, Camp Slasher, Quilt, Crawlspace, The Face of Midnight, Storberry, Shadow Witch, and the horror anthology, The Island. He lives in upstate New York with his beautiful wife, Terri, and their children, Joe, and Julia. Dan is a meteorologist with NOAA's National Weather Service. Besides writing, he enjoys visiting amusement parks, beach vacations, Renaissance fairs, gardening, playing with the family dogs, and eating ice cream.

Visit Dan at: www.danpadavona.com

The Redeemer

The Redeemer

Made in the USA
Monee, IL
17 July 2022

99898269R00073